God's Unwelcomed Wrath

THE RAPTURE

A novel about the end times,
the last days before the second coming.

ADAM GAMBILL

THE RAPTURE

God's Unwelcomed Wrath

Adam Gambill

Christian Publishing House

Cambridge, Ohio

Professional Christian Publishing of the Good News

Unless otherwise stated, Scripture quotations are from *The Holy Bible, Updated American Standard Version*®, copyright © 2017 by Christian Publishing House, Professional Christian Publishing of the Good News. All rights reserved.

THE RAPTURE: God's Unwelcomed Wrath by Adam Gambill

ISBN-13: 978-1-945757-58-7

ISBN-10: 1-945757-58-2

Table of Contents

CHAPTER 1 Flight from Danger

Running, as fast as I can. I don't know how much longer I can take it. At this point, I really do not have any other choice. I can turn around and head back home and risk getting caught, or I can continue on towards Garbor. It is the last place for people like me, for people who haven't yet taken the mark of the beast.

All of my family except my uncle disappeared several months ago, leaving me to try and figure out what happened to them. And while I'm still not one hundred percent for sure, I believe they were Raptured out. My uncle Rex has already taken the mark of the beast. Three perfectly aligned sixes now tattoo his right hand, allowing him to buy or sell with ease. And from what I saw before I left home recently, very few people now exist who haven't taken the mark.

While I don't have much going for me right now, I do have high hopes of making it to Garbor. Sure, I don't know where it is, but I intend to find it. I have no map, no money, only the clothes I wear and a solid gold pocket watch that I managed to hide from the Servants of Darkness. That is what the agents who search for new converts to Satanism call themselves. They are the ones who tattoo the mark of the beast on either your forehead or your right hand.

Before I went into hiding recently to avoid having to confront the choice of taking the mark or losing my life, I saw on the news where a man called Vladimir has taken control of much of the New World Order, called Wertenland. He wears white robes and calls himself the savior of the world. And unfortunately, most people have pledged their allegiance to him by taking his mark. I still can't get over the fact that my uncle took the mark. I tried hard to convince him to come with me, but he said it was "a fool's journey." Instead, he sold his soul to the devil, without any hope of ever making it to heaven. At least that's what my mom and all the other Christians used to say. As for me, I think I believe them.

If I have to, I can resort to using my pocket watch to buy information or food. I don't want to as it is the last thing I own apart from my clothes, but I may have to. The watch belonged to my father, and I barely managed to get it before the Servants of Darkness searched my home and gave me three months' time to either take the mark or give up my life.

I see movement ahead of me. I hunker down. I'm still only a few miles from home, so the Servants of Darkness have a strong presence throughout this area. I hope once I get far enough away from home, that I can travel without so much anxiety.

From the best I can tell, a group of children is playing around an old park, remnants of a better life. I have no doubt that they have taken the mark. What I cannot seem to understand is why some children were left behind, while most of them are no longer on the earth. I always heard mom say that all children would be taken home to heaven during the Rapture. I guess she was wrong. The thing is, I'm not exactly for sure the Rapture has happened, but I have a good idea that is has. But why now? Why would God decide several months ago to come and take his children home whenever the world seemed to be so much better off spiritually speaking. I mean, before so many people disappeared, there were revivals and people coming to the saving knowledge of Jesus Christ right and left.

I squint my eyes to try to see if I recognize any of the children. I do not. While they would probably turn me in if they saw me acting strangely, I still stand a chance of getting away without getting caught.

I decide to stay among the trees as I make my way around the park. The last thing I want right now is for a flock of agents to descend on me.

I swallow hard. I feel a drop of sweat slide down the middle of my back. I have to do this, I have to get away from here.

It's weird how some things, like the park, haven't changed when so many things have. A year ago, I never would have believed that things could get so bad, that things could go south so quickly.

I look at the ground while I make my way through the trees. I can't afford to get snake bit, and here lately, snakes are on the move. Nor can I afford to get sick, period.

I take shallow, nervous breaths as I watch the area for any signs of other people. I have heard of so many people getting caught trying to escape these past several months. And usually, when it comes down to it, most of the people who get caught take the mark of the beast rather than facing imminent death.

I wipe the sweat out of my eyes with the back of my hand. I feel like a stranger in a strange land. As many times as I have visited this park in the past, it feels so off limits right now, so wrong.

I can hear the children's voices fading away as I move further and further away from the park. It is so eerie now, so unpleasant. As much as I want to get away, I will miss seeing people, at least for a while. I hope Garbor is as nice as I've heard it is. It would be so disappointing to get there and learn that it was just a trick or something. And since I have staked my life on making it there, it better be everything I hope it is.

I'm now far enough away from the park, far enough away from Town, that I can breathe a sigh of relief. It is unlikely to meet someone this far out. Most of the agents tend to stay in the Towns. Of course, that doesn't mean that I won't run into one of them, but it means that it is less likely.

I have been on the move for more than an hour now. I am officially in the Outlands. The problem that I am going to have is to make it through all the Towns on my way to Garbor without getting caught. The only thing I know about Garbor is that it is a haven of refuge for religious people that is located somewhere in the Rocky Mountains. And from the best I can tell, I am somewhere between the east coast and the Midwest right now.

I stop and take in my surroundings. Everything seems so peaceful here, so wonderful compared to the Town I came from. Giant oak trees tower over the ground, casting their shadows of shade in pleasant places. I consider sitting under one of the trees, but I want to get farther away before I stop for an extended rest.

I'm going to have to find some water soon. I wish that I could have had time to get a bottle before leaving. I wish I weren't so scatter brained before I left. I hope I can find a clean stream of water to drink from. Most of the streams around here are murky with environmentally unfriendly runoff, rendering the water unfit to drink.

I take a deep breath and start moving again. Although I am not familiar with every tree and every plant here, I do know where about I am at. Best I can tell, I am on the verge of making it into the next county. This is good news since County Harrington is more rural than the one I am about to leave behind.

I wish that I had lived in the country and had more experience with roughing it. As silly as it may sound, I have little experience with the Outlands. I do know that there are rumors of people living underground in the country to avoid detection. That sounds good and all, but it will make it harder to get where I am going if I cannot talk to someone sensible.

I practically hug the trees for cover as I continue making my way through this wooded area. I spot a mushroom. I bend down and pick it.

I sniff it and then throw it down. It is a holly heart by the smell of it. They are poison. I know that there are edible mushrooms that look like holly heart, but I can't remember if they grow this time of year. Unfortunately, it is in the middle of August, one of the hottest months.

I had eaten all I could before I left Town, but it wasn't much. I had some stale bread that I scavenged from a dumpster, along with a swig of sour milk that I am sure made me frown, but nothing protein laden. I need to get some protein in me if I am to have the energy to make it across the country.

I hear an airplane somewhere high above me. I let out an annoyed breath. How nice it must be to be able to sit while traveling. Instead, I am on the move like a hobo.

It won't be long, and I will have to find somewhere safe to spend the night. It is too dangerous to travel at night, especially since I am an illegal. Yeah, I am an illegal in my own country. It is crazy.

I find a group of cane poles by a small stream. I decide to make a spear. Maybe I can spear me a fish for dinner. I should have left Town early in the morning, but I would have been in greater danger of getting caught. Since the shift change occurs before dawn, there are twice as many agents on the move as there are at any other time of the day.

I find a jagged rock that I use to sharpen the end of the cane pole. I use to watch shows on television where people would spear fish. And since I have little survival knowledge, I really don't know any other way to do it that doesn't involve hooks, worms, and fishing line.

About ten minutes later, I have a sharp spear ready to use. I carefully make my way down the river bank and search the water for any sign of life.

Nothing.

Instead of crossing the stream and getting my clothes wet, I decided to follow the stream until I can find a place to cross. Before no time at all, I spot a blackberry bush growing alongside the stream. I run up to it, seeing both red and black berries hanging on the thorny branches.

I start grabbing the blackberries and stuffing them into my mouth. They are so good. I haven't eaten blackberries in years. The last time I had blackberries was when I visited my cousins' farm many years ago.

When I finally get my fill of berries, I pick up my spear and set off again downstream. I hear squirrels barking at me as I make my way down the bank of the stream. I wish I had some way of getting a squirrel. The thing is, I have no gun or any other suitable weapon on me. I might as well eat worms. Then again, berries are better than worms any day.

I roll the round shaft of the spear in my hand as I nervously bide my time. I have a bad feeling about this, about heading off into the unknown. If only I had a map.

I spot a large dead tree ahead. I make my way towards it. It has a large opening at its base. I thank God for dead trees with openings. This will do.

I bend down and head inside the tree. Decayed wood fragments litter the ground from inside the tree. I look for beetles but don't see any. A big fat juicy beetle would have at least satisfied some of my protein needs.

Disappointed, I lay on my back and slowly begin to let my guard down. Before long, I feel myself drifting off to sleep.

I wake with a start. Somewhere close is a group of people's voices. I listen close for any sign of gender. It sounds like there are two women and a man.

I press my back against the inside of the tree, hoping I don't get discovered.

I turn my ear towards the approaching voices. Oddly enough, these people do not seem to be concerned about getting caught, which leads me to believe that they are indeed agents, Servants of Darkness, that is.

I listen closer. No, they can't be. I swallow hard, feeling caught between crawling closer to the entrance of the tree and staying put where I know I am safe.

I stiffen. Whoever this is, they just keep getting closer and closer. I pick up my spear. It is my only weapon.

"We can stay here tonight," says one of the women. "This is a good place to watch for fugitives."

I half consider crawling out of the tree, but I think it is too late.

Someone shines a light in my face.

"Someone's here," says the same women.

"What do you mean someone's hear," says another voice.

The woman shines the flashlight in my face. "I mean that there is a young man right here at the entrance to this tree."

I scrunch my face up, feeling stupid. Why didn't I stay all the way inside the back of the tree?

I find myself looking directly into the eyes of a slouched woman. She frowns, checking me out. "Who are you?" she says with a hateful tone.

I swallow hard. She is an agent. Dang it.

The man steps into the light. His eyebrows pulled together with a frown. I get the impression that he has seen me before.

I have two choices. I can either try to bolt for it or turn myself in.

The lady shines the light between my face and my hands. Then she smiles maliciously. "I have an unregistered!"

The other woman bends down to have a good look at me. She smiles too. "That he is, but where did he come from and where is he going."

I look at the clothes of all three of them. There is no doubt in my mind that they are agents. I half consider throwing a handful of rotten wood chips into their faces, but I doubt I could get far.

The man hunkers down and extends a hand towards me. I know what he wants. He wants to see my registration card, but I do not have one. Only those people who take the mark of the beast have a registration card. A registration card is what agents use to see where you came from, how old you are, and most importantly, your name.

I stare at his outstretched hand. I look between the three people. Each of them looks very pleased with themselves.

So I am caught. I shake my head and let out a defeated breath. I thought I would at least make it further than this before getting caught.

The prettier woman, with blond hair and blue eyes, looks at me carefully. She turns to her companions. "He looks more startled than a deer in headlights."

The man nods in agreement. He pulls his hand back from me. "From the looks of him, I don't think he has any valuables on him."

The blond haired woman looks at me with an *I'll see about that expression.* She looks down at my pants pockets. "Let's see it."

I swallow hard. "See what," I say.

She points at one of my bulging pockets. "Whatever you are carrying on you. Let me have it."

I'm beginning to get the impression that these three people are more concerned with the contents of my pockets than they are with me. I look between them. "No," I say defiantly.

The man points a pistol at my head. "I'm afraid I must insist."

I take a deep breath. As I let it out slowly, I reach for my watch inside my pocket. I take it out.

I hold it by the chain, looking at their facial expressions.

The man holds out his hand. "Hand it over."

I offer it to him. He takes it without a moment's hesitation.

As soon as he takes the watch into his hand, he shoves the gun back into its holster. I bristle.

He looks at the watch like it was Christmas. "Just what I've been looking for. This ought to buy us at least a month's worth of food."

I narrow my eyes on him. "A month's worth of food," I whisper. I am beginning to see that something is very wrong here. "Who are you?"

He grins. "Surely you do not expect me to throw my name around these days."

I roll my eyes. I guess not, but I had at least hoped that he would have given me some useful information.

I watch in anger as the man stuffs my pocket watch into his pants pocket. From the looks of his pockets, he already has a hoard of stuff in them.

He gives me a half satisfied look. "Is that all you have?"

I nod.

"Fine," he says. "Then we'll be on our way."

I narrow my eyes on him. Something weird is going on here, and I intend to figure it out. "Wait," I say. "Where are you going?"

The other woman, who has dark hair, looks me straight in the eyes. "That's none of your business."

I try to look brave. "Oh. So you take the only thing I own other than my clothes and won't even tell me why."

The man steps forward, takes the flashlight, and then shines it in my face. "You should feel lucky that we're not turning you in. We could you know."

I swallow hard. He's just trying to intimidate me. I give him a hard look.

He almost smiles. "Ah, don't like me, eh? All well, just be glad I didn't shoot you in the head and then take your watch."

The dark haired woman looks suddenly sympathetic. "Don't terrorize him, Jake."

The man turns around and gives her a scolding look.

The blond haired woman, who appears to be about twenty or so, extends a hand to me.

I take it. She pulls me to my feet.

"There," she says, looking pleased. She slowly turns to face Jake. "Don't listen to a word he says, I never do."

I can't help but laugh.

Jake turns on me with a cool look. "Well, since you know my name now, what's yours?"

I hesitate giving it to him. Instead, I simply shake my head.

The blond haired woman looks on me with a smile. She extends a hand to me. "I'm Donna, Donna Wells. It's nice to meet you."

I carefully meet her hand with my own. Since she is being so polite, I see no reason to withhold this information. "Kevin. Kevin Trill."

She smiles, squeezes my hand.

The dark haired woman steps up to me and extends a hand. "And I'm Leslie. Please forgive me for not giving you my last name, but I hate it."

I nod, thinking I understand her. If she is in the same situation that I am in, I can understand her wanting to leave her last name behind her. Last names can be used to identify you, which is why I am surprised Donna gave hers to me.

Donna seems to be catching on. "Oh, well, I'm not as worried as these two." She looks between Jake and Leslie. "If I die for refusal to take the mark of the beast, then I'll just end up in heaven, so, nothing to worry about."

Jake gives her a hard look. "Not everyone wants to wind up in heaven this soon. You do realize what you've done, don't you? All this time we've been doing well, and you had to go and ruin it."

Donna rolls her eyes. She looks at me and then back at Jake. "He's harmless." She turns back to face me. "What, you can't be more than sixteen, can you?"

8

I don't know why she thinks my age is so important considering I'm almost as tall as she is. Still, I nod.

Donna looks pleased with herself. She gives Jake a haughty look, runs a hand through her hair. "See, he's just a child."

I don't like to be called a child, but since Donna is treating me well, I don't want to go and ruin it. So, I decided to keep my mouth shut.

Leslie gives me an appraising look. "We could take him with us. Otherwise, he risks getting caught by a lot much worse than ours."

Donna claps her hands together. "What an excellent idea Leslie. Let's put it to a vote. Those in favor of taking Kevin with us say I, those opposed, keep your mouth shut."

Jake lets out a defeated breath. "Fine, but if he gives us away, I swear to God I'll shoot him in the head."

Donna's mouth falls open. She gives Jake a disdainful glare. "Why do you always have to be so hateful? Honestly, I think we'd be better off without you."

Jake snorts a laugh. "Yeah right, you don't even know how to shoot this gun."

Donna looks argumentative. "I could learn."

"Not if I take it with me," Jake says.

Leslie looks between the two of them. "Would you two stop fighting? Good grief, you'll have every Agent of Darkness within a two-mile radius on our tails."

I frown. I get the impression that these three are not from around here. From what I gleaned over the last several months, only people from the extreme northeastern districts call the bad guys Agents of Darkness. Everyone else calls them Servants of Darkness or just agents. Well, not everyone, but at least those who haven't yet taken the mark of the beast.

Leslie looks me over. She then turns to face Donna and Jake. "He might just come in handy if we were to need some extra help." Leslie bends down, picks up my spear. "For instance, anyone who can make something like this could become a good team member."

"Fine," Jake snaps. "But if he gets us caught, I'll pray to God to strike you down."

Leslie laughs. She turns to face me. "How do you like it? Do you think you could put up with the three of us?"

I look between the three of them. I consider my options. If I go with them, then I will feel safer, as well as have someone to help look out for me. But if I go it alone, then I stand less chance of getting caught. Three fugitives on the run are far more suspicious than one, even despite their attire. Then again, Jake has a gun, so that counts for something.

I nod. "Sure, I'll go with you all."

Leslie looks like she could kiss me. "Great! I think you'll find us three better families than those you left behind."

"Or those who left him behind," Jake says with a serious gleam in his eyes.

I swallow hard. Jake has a point. If only I had believed in God, I wouldn't be in this mess, to begin with. If only I accepted Jesus Christ as my Lord and Savior, instead of rolling my eyes every time my mom tried to convert me...

Jake shuts the flashlight off. He looks up at the sky. "We need to get moving. I won't be happy until we are miles away from here." He lowers his gaze to me, dark eyes cautious in the moonlight. "Bring your spear and anything else you may be hiding."

I nod. Leslie hands me the spear, looking triumphant.

I watch as Jake's cautious eyes scan the area for any sign of agents.

He looks between the three of us. "Let's go, and remember to be quiet." He looks at me until I nod, an unspoken contract.

With that said, Jake sets off on a run. In a split second, I watch as Donna and Leslie follow. I follow suit.

As we wind around the trees, I am tempted to ask Jake where we are going, but know better than to do so. He would probably punch me in the face or something. Out of all three of them, he is the least friendly.

What feels like several hours pass, leaving my leg muscles sore and aching. I wish I knew where we are going. I am trusting Jake to lead us in the right direction, though I could probably do better on my own. But then again, there is safety in numbers. I think. At least everyone is dressed like an agent. They could easily fool an agent, saying that I am a prisoner or something.

Jake starts slowing down, which is music to my ears, or should I say calf muscles. I just want to sit down and ask them how they managed to make it this far away from the extreme most northeast. In the Old Country, I believe they would have come from somewhere around Maine.

Jake points to a bridge just ahead. I let out a sigh of relief. I have wanted to cross this stream for ages. I don't know why, but part of me feels like we'll be a lot safer on the other side of the stream. Maybe Garbor isn't so far away from here.

Jake stops and stares at a sign at the bridge. It says that there is a ten thousand dollar reward for fugitives fleeing in this direction.

Jake takes something out of his pocket and unfolds it. A map!

I can hardly believe my eyes. I crowd among the three of them and stare at the map. I feel my heart sink. Half of the map has been torn off.

Jake gives me a knowing look. "I found this in a trash can the other day. I take it that whoever threw it away didn't want anyone finding their way to Garbor."

I nod. Dang it. I was excited for a split second. I look between the three of them. "So, what good is half a map?"

Jake looks at me like I am stupid. "Because half of a map is better than none at all. And because I have enough stuff in my pockets to more than bribe a person to give us a complete map."

Leslie nods, then looks at me. "He isn't lying. Take that gold pocket watch, for instance, it could get us just the kind of rare artifact that we need."

I let out a disgruntled sigh. "Maybe so, but as for myself, I'd rather have the pocket watch."

Jake looks at me like I am an idiot. "Why? What better use could you have for a pocket watch other than buying us the information we need to get where we're going."

I can see the logic in his reasoning. "Yeah, I guess so. It's just that that pocket watch is the last thing I own that belonged to my father."

Jake looks sympathetic. "Hey, maybe we won't have to use it. If we don't, I'll give it back to you."

"You will," I say, hearing how stupid I sound.

Jake nods. "Sure, if I don't have to use it, I won't."

I nod. Jake doesn't seem as bad as I had originally thought.

"So," I begin, wanting to know more about these three. "Where exactly did you all come from anyway, if you don't mind me asking?"

Jake sets off across the bridge, a look of determination in his eyes. "Namsor. About as far north as you can go."

11

Namsor. Hmm. "I've never heard of Namsor before."

Donna looks taken aback. "You haven't? Jeeze, I thought everyone has heard about Namsor before. After all, it was the first district that began chopping off the heads of those who refused to take the mark of the beast."

I swallow hard. "Really?"

Donna nods. "Yup, and just a few months ago. We," she says, looking between Leslie and Jake, "decided to leave as soon as the beheadings occurred. We've been on the move ever since."

I frown. "You mean you've been traveling this much ever since then."

Leslie shakes her head. "No, just off and on. We would take refuge at safe spots along the way until some of the locals would rat us out. And then we would be on our way again."

We leave the bridge behind. Jake motions us to step over into the wooded area, probably for safety concerns.

I look at Leslie. "So, let me get this straight. You three have been traveling together for the last several months?"

Each of them nods, one by one. Jake takes out a registration card. He hands it to me. I take it and look it over. I feel my jaw drop.

I look at Jake. "This is an agent's card. How'd you get it?"

Jake considers this. "Well, I didn't find it just laying around. Oh," Jake says, catching on, "I didn't kill anyone for it either. I stole it. Whenever the agent wasn't looking, I swiped it."

Donna looks like she could bounce up and down in happiness. She looks at Jake. "Tell him the rest of the story. He deserves to know."

Jake nods, takes the card back from me. "There really isn't much to tell. I took the card from a senior agent while his back was turned to me. I knew he was an important official from the way he was dressed. He had several rows of stripes on his shirt, making me want to swipe his card all the more."

I frown. I shake my head. "But why would an agent, especially a senior agent leave his registration card laying around?"

Jake gives me a mischievous smile. "Because, when he told me to get in line for the mark of the beast, I asked him where his authority came from. Next second, he took out his wallet, pulled out his card, and showed it to me. After that, Donna turned on the charm. She," he says, grinning, "well, she flicked her hair this way and that until the agent unwittingly set his card on the table in front of him, while pushing his wallet back into his pocket. When his back was turned, I took it."

I smile. That was one of the best stories I ever heard. "That's awesome. And now you are him."

Jake nods. "Yup, I am an Agent of Darkness, ready to authorize the decapitation of countless innocents."

Donna rolls her eyes. "You should just be thankful that you weren't caught." She faces me. "Anyone else and it would not have worked."

Leslie nods in agreement, looking a bit sad. She looks between Jake and Donna. "Oh, so you two did all the work did you? So you must mean that I just stood aside and let you both do everything?" She looks daggers at Jake. She points an angry finger at him. "Just for your information, if it weren't for me, you would have never been able to take that card, to begin with."

Leslie turns to me. "You see, I was the one who distracted the other agents while all this took place. There were three other agents sitting at those tables, so I decided to start screaming in order to distract them from what Donna and Jake were about to do. But it seems that that one agent was more interested in Donna than hearing me scream."

I look between the three of them. I do feel a little sorry for Leslie. You'd have thought that Donna and Jake had pulled it off all by themselves, but truth be told, Leslie deserved recognition as well. I wonder why they left out Leslie from the story."

I get the impression that these three are not as close as I had originally thought. And that's not good. I just hope that Leslie lets it go and doesn't hold a grudge. Mom always said that holding a grudge was worse for you than it was for anyone else.

I incline my head at a log just ahead of us. Jake smiles, understandingly. Donna gives me an appreciative smile, perhaps for changing the subject. Still, I get the impression that there is something that they are not telling me about, and I intend to figure it out.

After resting for a couple of hours, I see an orange tinge in the sky, a sign that the sun isn't far behind.

I look at Jake. "So, where to from here?"

Jake gives me a sad look. "I guess we follow the map until we can't anymore." He takes the map out of his pocket and unfolds it. He shines the flashlight on it.

It's so confusing. I don't even know where we are in relation to the map. All there is is a bunch of lines and squiggly marks.

Donna presses a finger onto the map. "I think we are somewhere around here." Jake nods in agreement.

I see the Town where I am from, which is not far away. I feel my heart sink. "We're not as far away as I thought we were."

Leslie looks happy about this. Jake gives her a hard look.

"Well," Leslie says, "if I was leading us, we'd already be in another district instead of doddering around here in this one."

Jakes hard look turns even harder. "Oh, so you think you can do better than me? If you're not happy, no one is keeping you here."

Leslie looks like she wants to say something, but keeps her mouth closed instead.

Donna looks like she is on pins and needles. "We should find somewhere proper to rest. I don't like this area, it's too close to the road."

I nod. I look at the map again. The bad thing about this map is that it is not very detailed. Other than a few of the major roads, there is nothing else listed. I'm beginning to see why Jake was so happy to get my dad's pocket watch. We need all the information we can get.

Jake rises to his feet and shoves the map back into his pocket. He looks between Donna and I. "Best I can tell, we need to keep heading west. And since this road goes west, I say we stay as close to it as possible."

Leslie gives Jake a cool look since he did not look at her reaction. I can tell that this is going to be a fun adventure.

Jake turns off the flashlight and then offers it to me. I take it from him. The last thing I want is to have to carry something around feeling so tired, but since I am now a part of this group, I feel responsible to do everything I can to help.

Jake sets off parallel to the road while staying in the woods. I hope we find some place to rest soon because I am worn out.

After walking another hour or two, we finally happen across an old shed of some sort. From the looks of it, no one has lived around here for ages, making it a good place to rest.

I prepare myself for a long deserved rest, but Jake walks right past it.

I stop and clear my throat. Jake turns towards me.

I incline my head at the shed. "What's wrong with it? I mean, there's obviously no one around."

Jake points a thumb over his shoulder. "It's too close to the highway. We need to find somewhere more discreet."

I feel like hanging my head in disappointment. That was the last thing I wanted to hear.

Jake almost smiles, as if sensing my thoughts. "We'll find somewhere better than this, just wait."

I feel like telling him that I have waited long enough, but I know he is right. So, I keep my mouth shut. Leslie, on the other hand, looks as if she refuses to wait for another second to let her voice be heard.

"I think this is the perfect place to stay," Leslie says. "Who would search an old shed out in the middle of nowhere?"

I can see Jake caving in, his facial expression turning annoyed. "Fine, but if I step on an old nail, I will expect you to pull it out. As for the location of this place, maybe we will be fine."

Leslie gives Jake a haughty look before offering me a nicer one. She leans into me as Jake heads towards the shed. "If he ever stepped on a nail, I'd be sure and drive it deeper into his foot."

I'm sure I look taken aback. That was an awful thing to say. I wonder why Leslie is even here since she obviously hates Jake so much.

I follow Donna into the shed. There doesn't appear to be any skunks, but it could still use a good cleaning. There's a table and chairs in the far corner, along with several tin cans on the floor.

Jake looks uneasy. "I don't know, maybe we should keep following that highway to see where it takes us. This isn't much of a place to stay anyway."

I laugh. If only my parents could see me now. I can hear their voices in my head. *You should have converted to Christianity long ago, and then you wouldn't be here. If only you had made Jesus the Lord of your life, then you'd be in heaven right now.*

Jake and Donna look at me like there is something wrong with me. Leslie, on the other hand, looks quite pleased as if she and I are going to become good friends.

I shrug. "I guess there could be worse places."

Jake looks around at the dilapidated shed. "Maybe, but I have yet to see any of them."

Donna points to something crumpled up in the corner of the room. "It looks like a tablecloth."

I head over to it to investigate. As silly as it may seem, even old tablecloths could come in handy when you have very little to your name.

I grab hold of one of the corners of the tablecloth and pull it towards me. I hear a hissing sound beneath the cloth.

"It's a opossum," Donna says with glee. She looks between Jake and me. "You know what this means, food!"

I can't help but give Donna a stupefied look. "A opossum? You want to eat a opossum?"

Donna runs over and grabs the opossum by the tail. "And it's an adult too. There ought to be enough food here to feed all of us." She turns to Jake. "What do you say?"

Jake shrugs. "Couldn't be any worse than eating snakes I suppose."

I narrow my eyes at him. "You've eaten snakes before?"

Jake nods. "Yup and they are delicious."

Yuck. The last thing I want to eat is a snake. Compared to a snake, I guess an opossum seems like a pretty sophisticated meal.

Donna holds the opossum out in front of her, careful to avoid getting bitten. She looks like she is salivating. She turns on me with a happy look.

"Ever had opossum before," Donna says.

I shake my head.

Donna smiles. "Then you are in for a real treat. Some people think they're better than chicken. As for me, I think they're a bit like a duck."

I give the opossum a pitied look. If only there were something else to eat besides a poor old opossum. Maybe we should look for a stream and catch some fish somehow.

Donna extends her free hand, silently requesting Jake's pistol. He gives it to her.

Leslie turns on Donna with a nasty look. "Surely you aren't stupid enough to shoot a gun around here. Do you actually think it won't be heard?"

Donna looks as if she is having second thoughts about shooting the opossum.

The cautious gleam in Jake's eyes shows that he agrees with Leslie, but is pulled between wanting to snub Leslie and letting Donna have her way.

Donna lowers the opossum to the floor. "I didn't think of that. I guess we'll have to eat something else."

The opossum runs to the nearest corner of the shed and disappears in a hole in the floor.

Donna hands the pistol back to Jake. As if there is an unspoken truce between each other, Jake turns around and heads towards the door.

I can tell that Jake would have liked to eat opossum, but he just didn't want to risk getting caught. And who could blame him?

I follow Jake out the door. It's just as well. It was too hot in that shed anyway. Donna emerges from the shed behind me, followed by Leslie.

"So," I begin, "where to now?"

"Into the unknown," Jake says. "Hopefully we can find somewhere better to rest for a while."

I nod. Donna gives me a friendly look. Leslie winks at me. I narrow my eyes at her. She's got to be at least twenty-five or thirty years old.

Jake continues heading west, glancing over his shoulder a couple of times to make sure that we are following him. I wish we could find some clean water before long, I'm thirsty.

I can't help but notice how worried Jake looks. Even with his stolen identification, he looks more uneasy than I feel.

I fall into step beside him as we enter another wooded area. I hear Donna and Leslie talking about the possum behind us. It sounds like Donna is ticked off at Leslie.

I glance sideways at Jake. "So, what's on your mind? You look troubled."

Jake meets my gaze with a worried look. "I was just thinking since nearly everyone alive has now taken the mark of the beast, there aren't going to be many people we can trust. It wasn't easy finding Donna and Leslie. The reason why we clicked right away is that none of us wanted to take the mark."

I consider this. "You make it sound like everyone is going to be against us. Just because they've taken the mark doesn't mean that they won't help us."

Jake looks at me like I've got it all wrong. "Most people would rather turn us in rather than help us. Haven't you heard about the new law? Anyone discovered helping people like us, that is people who haven't yet taken the mark, will be subject to cruel and unusual punishment."

He's right, I didn't know that. Still, there have to be some people left like us. I decide to run this by him.

Jake looks shocked that I did not know this. "Furthermore, the folks that haven't yet taken the mark are not exactly going to advertise it, are they? No, we're going to have to be extra careful about being seen anywhere and everywhere."

"Pray," Donna says, now beside me. "We need to pray that God spares us. Perhaps we can make it to Garbor. As for me, I'd be okay with just living with people like us, even if they're not in Garbor. But then again," Donna says with a look of mixed emotions, "the Agents of Darkness are only going to multiply and spread to all parts of the country. It won't be long, and it will be hard to just find any place of refuge other than Garbor."

I hear Leslie say something behind me, though I didn't understand her. "What," I say.

Leslie looks upbeat. "If we can just get out of this district, I think we stand a good chance of making it to Garbor. And if we don't, I'm sure that there'll be other safe havens along the way. I read something interesting in a newspaper not long ago. It was estimated that over a million people do not intend to take the mark of the beast."

I swallow hard. "Is that all? I mean, surely there are more people than that who want to go to heaven."

Leslie shrugs. "Maybe, but a million people is not a small number."

Donna chimes in. "It is when you consider that there are more than two hundred million people living in the country."

Jake nods. "That's right. It still baffles me when I think of how many people have received the mark. I figured that millions more would have held out, but they didn't. It's like all the people wanted to lose their souls or something. It's crazy."

I think of something. I look at Jake. "Do you know how many people reside in Garbor?"

Jake shakes his head. "No, and as bad is it will sound, I don't even know if Garbor even exists."

I take a deep breath. "But it has to. I mean, if it doesn't, then we'll have journeyed there for nothing."

Donna looks hopeful. "I wouldn't get too depressed just yet. From what I heard before I fled from home was that Garbor was expanding its walls to add more people. I think it's still there, waiting for us."

It sounds great. I can't wait to be around other people like us, that is people who haven't taken the mark.

That reminds me of something. I turn to Jake. "Hey, about your stolen registration. Is there a picture on it?"

Jake looks relieved. "No, otherwise I would not have taken it."

Well, that's a relief.

I take a long look at Jake. From the looks of him, he can't be more than three or four years older than me. I consider asking him his age, but I hear something off in the distance drawing closer.

"Get down," Jake says.

I hunker down, trying to see the highway through all the trees. Whatever is coming is going very slow.

"It's an old car," Leslie says, whispering. She rises to her feet. She takes off running towards the highway. I can hear her shouting at the car.

Jake curses, staying down.

"She'll give us away," Donna says, looking worried.

We wait quietly for what feels like several minutes. I can't see much going on, just a blurred image of the car through the trees. I half consider crawling to get a closer look, but I see someone coming closer.

"It's Leslie," Donna says. "Does she have someone with her?"

"No," Jake says, rising to his feet. "She's alone."

As soon as Leslie appears, Jake walks up to her and slams the palm of his hand onto her chest. Leslie tumbles backward to the ground. "What was that? Huh, what was that? Do you have a death wish?"

I look in the direction of the car, afraid that whoever is over there will hear us.

Donna looks like she wants to chew Leslie up and spit her out. I can tell that she's about to shout. "What were you thinking? Who's over there, an agent?"

Leslie puts a hand on her ribcage. "No, just a middle aged man. I knocked him out, don't know how much longer he'll be out."

Jake looks ready to crucify Leslie. "Do you have any idea what you done, what could have happened? And you know my policy, no brutality. So, you better have a real good excuse, or I'm cutting you out of this group."

Leslie rises to her feet. She looks Jake right in the eyes. "I hate you. I hate you for putting us through all this. I haven't had any sleep in three days, plus my legs are killing me. What do you expect? That I'd walk all the way to Garbor when it's likely still hundreds of miles away?"

Jake nods, dark eyes angry. "Yes. If you're going to get along with us, then you're going to have to think like us. What you did was stupid. You could have easily got all of us captured."

I look at Donna. I have never seen her look this angry before. She looks as if she could drive Leslie into the ground like a hammer.

Jake flicks his eyes to the car. "It's too risky. There are bound to be checkpoints every few counties. I just don't see it working."

Leslie massages her shoulder. "It shouldn't be a problem. After all, you do have a senior agent's registration card. And on top of that, you're reasonably intelligent."

Jake scoffs. "You're the first person I've ever known who could lie with such ease. Nevertheless, you made a good point. Plus, I don't want to have to walk any more than I have to. Walking takes energy, and we don't have any food."

I let out a deep breath. I hadn't realized I was holding my breath. Still, I'm glad that Jake has decided to take the car. I'm not sure I could take roughing it much longer."

Jake waves a hand in front of him, dark eyes harder than ever. "Lead the way. And you'd best hope that that man doesn't remember what you look like when he wakes up."

Leslie leads the way to the car. I just hope that we can get in the car and head west before any agents show up. It's one thing to fool someone who isn't an agent, but it's another to try to fool an agent. I just hope that we never have to try.

As soon as we leave the woods behind, it feels at least five degrees hotter. Jake walks around the car and sizes everything up.

Jake points to the ditch beside the road. "Someone will need to drag him over there out of the way."

I nod. "I'll do it." Jake nods his consent.

I put my hands up under the man's armpits and drag him away from the car. Next, I pull him down the bank and into the ditch.

"Kevin, let's go," Jake says in a hurried voice.

I jog back up the bank and stop by the car. Jake motions for me to get in the backseat, so I do.

Donna situates herself in the passenger seat, leaving Leslie to sit by me. At least Leslie hasn't shown any aggression towards me, but I'd still rather sit by Donna. She's easier to confront and would probably be more likely to answer my questions.

Leslie shoots me a half haughty, half friendly look as if she would like to hear a thank you for getting us this vehicle. I decide not to oblige her.

Jake turns the car around and heads west. Ever since I left home, I have attributed heading west to freedom. If we can just ride for an hour or two, I'll be happy.

I lean forward to see how much gas is in the car. "Over half a tank," I say.

Jake nods, keeping his eyes on the road. "Anything less and I'd give Leslie a real scolding."

Leslie rolls her eyes. I hear her mumble something under her breath that sounds like *I dare you to try.*

I just hope that we don't run into any agents on the road. I feel sleep taking me under, my eyelids growing heavier and heavier.

CHAPTER 2 The Earthquake

"Wake up," Jake says, gently shaking me. "We found a good place to rest a few hours."

I sit up, wiping the sleep from my eyes. "Where are we?"

Jake turns around and points at his map. "Norfolk. And I think there's a good lake where we can fish."

"Sounds good," I say, stifling a sigh.

Jake grins. "I parked the car around the back side of the house. I've already been inside, no one's home. It looks like it's been abandoned for years. Still, there are a few old blankets that we can sleep on."

I open the door and get out of the car. I stretch and yawn at the same time. Jake runs a hand through his hair, trying to adjust to the lake breeze.

"Let's go," Jake says. "We could all use some sleep."

I look between Donna and Leslie. Both of them look years older than they are due to sleep deprivation.

Leslie yawns. "So, we'll sleep now and eat later."

Jake nods. "That's the plan."

And it sounds like a good one to me.

I follow Jake and Donna into the house. Leslie says she's going for a drink of water from the lake before she lays down.

I take in the pitiful shape of the house. The curtains look like torn rags hanging from rods, while the floor has large holes in it. It looks like the termites took this place over a long time ago.

Jake walks around the weak spots and motions for us to follow him. I'm just glad that no one is here. I wonder how long this place has been abandoned.

Jake leads us down a short hallway and into another room. I quickly spot the blankets that Jake mentioned earlier. And from the looks of them, someone has been here fairly recently.

Jake bends down and picks up a blanket. He hands it to me.

I shake the dust off of it. I let out a loud yawn. As dangerous a stunt as it was for Leslie to procure us a vehicle, I have to admit, I don't know if we would be here now if she hadn't.

Screaming. I look out the window but can't see anything through the dirty panes. Jake runs out of the room, dodging the holes in the floor as he goes.

"Get down," Jake says, standing in the doorway. "I'll go and see what's happened."

I swallow hard. It sounded like Leslie got snake bit or something. I hope she's alright.

I half consider running after Jake just in case he needs any help, but Donna pulls on my jeans, motioning me to hunker down. So I do.

Minutes go by and there is still no sign of Jake or Leslie. I decide to leave the safety of this room in search of them.

I hear a gunshot ring out as soon as I rise to my feet. Since Jake was the only one with a gun, I wonder what has happened.

I look at Donna. "I've gotta go," I say. She nods. I run out of the room, dodging all the bad spots on the floor like Jake did earlier.

I make my way down the hallway, my mind flooding with terrible thoughts.

I finally make it to the front door. I can already see Leslie on the front porch. And someone else lying in a pool of blood.

It is Jake.

"He's dead," I say, more to myself.

Leslie smiles. "Yes, the stupid little creep didn't realize that I was just leading him to his death."

I feel my jaw drop. "It was you. I mean, you set him up."

Leslie nods. "Let's just say that I got tired of him giving all the orders."

I stare at the pistol in Leslie's hand. I can't believe it. Jake is dead.

In a wave of anger, I lunge at Leslie, intent on knocking the gun from her hand.

But it goes off.

I double over, feeling a bloody hole in my stomach. I cry out, then crumple over.

I feel someone shaking me. "Wake up," says a voice vaguely familiar. But it can't be. Jake is dead. "Wake up, you're having a nightmare or something."

I wake up, alone in the car. The door is open, and Jake is hunkered down beside me, a worried gleam in his eyes.

I take a good look at his head. "Oh thank God," I say. "You're alive."

Jake looks slightly taken aback. "Of course I'm alive. Look, you've just been dreaming. Come on, I've found a good place to rest for a day or two."

I let out a sigh of relief.

I leave the car behind and soon find myself in the afternoon sun. It is hot, and I am thirsty.

Jake gives me an impatient look. "Come on, you're not going to believe what we found."

I can't help but feel curious. "What did you find?"

"Come on and I'll show you," Jake says.

Jake leads me to what appears to be an old abandoned house nestled among a bunch of oak trees. At least it doesn't look as bad as the shed did earlier. With a good coat of paint and some work done on the roof, this house could be livable again.

I look around for a lake, a remnant of a bad dream. At least this is a wooded area. It will be harder for an agent to find us way out here. From the looks of it, we are miles and miles from civilization.

I follow Jake up the steps to the front porch. He turns around and gives me a funny look. "I wish you'd hurry up. If you don't, Donna and Leslie are liable to eat everything before you get there. As for me, I've already eaten one can of tuna."

Yuck. But then again, I guess I shouldn't be so picky, considering that I'm on the run and have no means of supporting myself.

I enter the house cautiously. I blame the dream I had earlier for that.

Jake leads me around what appears to be some weak spots in the floor. I am careful to follow in his footsteps.

"The kitchen is through here," Jake says, leading me across the living room.

When I enter the kitchen, I see Donna and Leslie sitting at an old table, with several tin cans opened around them.

Donna motions for me to sit down opposite her. "You're not going to believe the food we found in here. There's enough to last us a week."

I look at the cans on the table. I see cans of tuna, beans, and potatoes.

Leslie hands me a manual can opener. I go for a can of potatoes.

"So," I say, happy that there's something other than tuna to eat, "where do you all think the owners ran off to? I mean, why would someone just leave all this food behind, along with the house?"

Leslie considers this. "Well, from what we could tell, the occupants left in a hurry. There are still closets full of clothes and a pantry full of food, not to mention nice looking beds to sleep in."

Jake sits down next to me. He takes his map out and looks at it. He taps an area with a finger and then lays it down on the table.

"I don't think we should stay here much longer," Jake says. "As rural as this place seems, there's a reason why the owners left this place. And I don't like it. More than likely, they wanted to avoid taking the mark of the beast, or they went in the Rapture. As for me, I think they left on their own."

I frown. "What makes you think so?"

"I have proof," Jake says, reaching for a Bible on the table. "This was laying here when we came in. It was already opened to Revelation. But more specifically, it was opened to the chapter that talks about the number of the beast."

I feel my jaw drop. Wow. If that's true, then whoever lived here probably did miss the Rapture. I know I shouldn't feel this way, but at least I'm not the only one left behind.

I take a fork from a pile on the table and spear me a potato. I stuff it into my mouth. It is delicious.

"So," I say, chewing a potato chunk, "you think there's a good chance that whoever lived here headed for Garbor?"

Jake nods. "Yes, and I don't think it has been long since they left. From the looks of this place, it was recently dusted. I mean, I know it looks a bit run down and all, but I think that is how the house looked when its occupants lived in it. I think they missed the Rapture and fled as soon as they heard of a man called Vladimir rising to the stage of world history."

Leslie holds up a finger. "That all sounds good and everything, but I want to know why you think we have to leave as soon as possible."

"Because," Jake begins, looking irritable, "I think there are agents close by. So close that all this food and comfort has been passed up by people other than us."

"Wow," I say. "That's really good thinking. I agree."

Jake, who looks as if he could be my older brother, turns back to the map. He points to an area by a major highway. "I think we are somewhere around here. And if that's the case, then we should get a move on quick. I wouldn't be one bit surprised if an agent weren't heading this way right now. Since this highway is the primary one connecting two districts together, you can bet that it is going to be used by the Agents of Darkness."

I rise to my feet. That's enough for me. I look between the three of them. Donna is already packing food into a bag. Leslie, on the other hand, seems content to stay a little longer. I can tell that Jake is still irritated with her.

I grab a plastic bag off the table and begin helping Donna. She smiles a thank you at me. Even though I do not like tuna, I intend to help bag up every last can that there is. The last thing I want to do is get into another situation where we are forced to eat opossum.

I feel a stab of anxiety in my chest that wasn't there a few moments ago. We need to leave and fast. We cannot afford to get caught, despite Jake's false identification. I hurry to the car as fast as I can.

Jake says something behind me. I turn around and face him.

"No car," he says, gauging my reaction. "I'm sorry Kevin, but I should never have driven it here, to begin with. It's too dangerous. We need to stay off the highway."

I nod. That means that we'll have to carry all our new supplies by hand. And won't that be taxing?

Donna stands beside me, holding two bags stuffed with food and other supplies including the manual can opener.

Leslie is the last to leave the house. I watch in amazement as she leaves the front porch behind with twice as much stuff as Donna and I have.

"It's strange," Leslie says, coming to a stop beside me. "I feel guilty about taking the food, but I also feel guilty about having to leave some of it behind."

I laugh. "Yeah, I can see how that would be a problem."

Jake just shakes his head. He points to the area west of the house and sets off in that direction. We follow suit.

Well, at least no one got shot. Ever since I had that dream in the car, I've been afraid that perhaps it was from God or something. I remember several years ago, mom used to talk about God giving her dreams to warn her about stuff. And although she swore that He really did give her a few dreams, I simply wrote them off as ordinary.

I turn to Leslie. "Here, let me carry some of that." She hands me a bulging bag full of stuff.

I waste no time heading into the woods behind Jake. The last thing I want is for any one of us to get captured by agents.

I just wish I could have slept a few hours more. I feel like I could drop at any second. My legs ache, and now my arms are hurting under such heavy loads. I just hope the bags hold up.

Donna gives me a sympathetic look. "You know, you're really a good kid. I'm surprised that you didn't make the Rapture."

I want to laugh, but don't out of the seriousness of the conversation. "Thanks," I say. "I guess I wasn't the angel my mom hoped I'd be."

"Don't feel bad," Leslie says. "My parents used to tell me that if I didn't convert soon, they were going to give me up for adoption. Dad used to say that all that was standing between me and hell was a simple decision. Thing is, I didn't want to give up my drinking and cavorting just to prepare myself for the Rapture."

Jake lets out an exhaustive sigh.

I look at him. "What about you? What's your story?"

Jake gives me a sad smile. "Well, if you have to know, I never thought much about Jesus Christ. I mean, I thought he might be real, but what I really thought was that Christians just used God as an excuse to act holier than thou. The thing is, now they're all gone and here I am, still on the earth."

I can't help but feel sad. "Yeah, I know what you mean. Thing is, I never really thought much about church or Jesus Christ either. But if I can get through all this, even if it means losing my life, I intend on living my life for Jesus all the way."

"That's good," Donna says, now at my other side. She seems like a nice lady. "Even though I'm a little late, I've already accepted Jesus Christ as my Lord and Savior. You know, I think it says in the Bible that you can still be saved after the Rapture. And with Bible prophecy unfolding right and left here lately, I believe that God will save those who persevere to the end."

I hear Leslie snicker behind me. I cast a look at her over my shoulder. She looks like she is caught in the middle of wanting to believe in Jesus and wanting to live without taking the mark, just in case you can lose your soul.

I feel like I need to talk to Leslie, but I really don't feel comfortable with doing so right now. Instead, I just keep my mouth shut.

After what felt like days of walking, we finally make it to what looks like an abandoned Town.

Jake looks at me. "Says Yellowbrook on the map. According to the orange dot around it, it used to be a heavily populated area."

I scan the sky for skyscrapers, and when I don't see any, I assume that it is a smaller Town. Nevertheless, I can tell that Jake doesn't want to walk right into it. And he is smart to think like that.

Jake looks between the three of us. "I say we wait until dark and then head in. It's likely that someone will be at home, though they might not be friendly to us. If we could just get some solid information on Garbor, I'd feel a lot better myself."

I nod. Donna looks like I feel. As for Leslie, well, she looks like she ate sour grapes. If she dislikes being with us this much why doesn't she just leave? I know she doesn't agree with a lot of the decisions made by Jake. Thing is, Jake has a good, level head on him, which I think we all need in a leader.

Jake turns away from the Town and heads back into the woods. He sits his bag of food down and sits on a fallen tree. I sit beside him. Donna sits on his other side while Leslie sits next to me. For some reason, Leslie acts like she likes me more than the other two. That makes it harder on me when it comes to trying to avoid taking sides.

I look at Jake's side profile. He reminds me a lot of my cousin Lance. Lance was known for his good looks. He had high cheek bones and dark hair, among other attributes. Jake also reminds me a lot of an older brother. Even though he's not much older than I am, I can tell that he has qualities about him that much older men do not even have. And most importantly, he has intellect and a good dose of common sense.

I watch as the sun slowly makes its way towards the horizon. It won't be long now and we'll be heading into Town. I'm a little nervous, but also excited about the prospects of what information we may learn. If we can just find someone who has heard of Garbor, I'll be happy. For all I know, it may not even exist. After all, I've only ever heard stories about it. And that has been over the last few months since the Rapture.

I reach into one of my bags and pull out a bottle of water. I take a drink. I should ask Jake whether or not we will be taking all this stuff with us, or if we'll leave it and come back for it later. Thing is, I'm so tired that even talking now seems overly taxing. I need a nap before we head into Town.

Jake meets my eyes. "Let's go." He rises to his feet. He looks at our supplies. "Let's leave our stuff here so that, in the event we have to run, we won't be weighted down."

I nod. Donna looks as nervous as I feel. I turn to Leslie. She seems like she wants to say something, but is holding back for some reason. Honestly, if she wants to leave, I'd say farewell.

I glance at the pistol at Jake's waist. I wish we had more weapons, not that I want to use them, but because I'd feel more secure.

Jake looks between the three of us. "Stay behind me. If I say run, then run. If I say stop, then stop. If I say leave me and run for it, then do so. As for me, I will do everything I can to avoid having to use this gun. The last thing I want is to have to wound or kill someone. Now let's go."

I swallow hard. I hope we don't get caught. I stay right behind Jake. I glance over my shoulder. Donna and Leslie are right behind me. I'm hoping that we do not attract too much attention, though I'm sure the darkness with help us.

Jake leads us around the back side of a row of houses. Since I don't see any lights on, I assume that nobody is at home. There's no telling what we could find in these houses. Perhaps more food, or maybe something more valuable. But then again, I feel guilty about taking things that don't belong to me. The thing is, if many of these people went in the Rapture, then whatever is in their houses will eventually be confiscated by agents.

I look at the ground, careful not to trip over anything. Several big trees cast their shadows across the yards we are walking through. I wonder what Jake is looking for. I guess I should have asked him before we headed out.

As we slowly make our way across the yards, I can't help but wonder if we're being watched. It wouldn't surprise me one bit if an agent wasn't already on our tails. I wish I had eyes in the back of my head. But since I am in the middle, Jake and the others are more at risk than I am. And while I'm not necessarily happy about that, I do feel blessed.

I come to a stop behind Jake. He motions for me to come closer, so I do.

Jake hunkers down behind a big oak tree. "Something doesn't feel right. I don't know for sure, but I think we're being followed."

I look at the yard around us. "Yeah, I do to. Thing is, whoever it is hasn't descended on us yet, so maybe it's not an agent."

"Yeah," Jake says, dark eyes gleaming in the moonlight. "But that's not to say we aren't in trouble. You know as well as I do that agents pay good money for the capture of people like us."

I nod. Donna comes into view, followed by Leslie.

"What's wrong," Donna says. "Are we in trouble?"

Jake gives her a maybe so, maybe not look. "I think we'll be better off to leave this place behind as soon as possible."

Leslie considers this. "Maybe so, but I think we'd do well to try to find someone in this Town to talk to. Surely there's someone who has been left behind besides us. I mean besides an agent."

"Maybe so," Jake begins, "but I see no need to risk our lives just for information."

Donna chimes in. "How about this: if we can't find someone to talk to soon, then we leave. As for myself, I feel like there should be someone in this Town who can give us some answers."

Jake looks defeated. "Fine, but if we get caught or reported, don't get angry if I say I told you so."

I look at Jake's bulging pockets. I meet his eyes. "Don't forget, you have a fake ID if you need to use it."

Jake looks surprised he forgot this. "Yeah, I guess I do." He looks between us. "Alright, let's see what we can figure out. If all goes well, we should be able to make it back to our supplies well before dawn."

"Should we split up," I say.

Jake shakes his head. "No, let's stay together."

Within a few minutes we head up the steps to the front porch of an abandoned looking house. Donna suggested this house as it is large and likely to have things we need. Then, she said, we can try to find an occupied home. I can see her reasoning, because should we run into trouble, we'd likely leave the Town without having done much investigative work.

Jake opens the door and steps inside. I feel a chill run down my spine. This is just the kind of place to run into trouble. As a matter of fact, I'm just thankful that we didn't run into any trouble at the last place we stopped.

Jake motions for Donna to give him the flashlight. As there are few windows in this house, it is extra dark.

"Be careful where you step," Jake says, dark eyes cautious. "Before we set out, I heard stories of agents setting booby traps to try to catch the Undecided."

I frown. "Undecided?"

Jake nods. "That's what people who are unsure of whether or not they want to take the mark of the beast are called. As for people like us, well, we're called the Undesirables. That's because we refuse to take the mark of the beast. With us, there's no question of whether or not to take the mark, we have already made up our minds. So, you can see why the Undecided are valued more than we are."

I nod, understanding. I'm surprised I hadn't already heard about the strange names.

Jake puts a finger to his mouth, wanting silence.

We slowly make our way through the house, careful to watch where we step. I hear the floor creak everywhere Donna steps. Donna is much heavier than the rest of us, so that doesn't surprise me.

I look at the stairway. It appears to be in fine shape. From the looks of this house, it hasn't been long since it was lived in. Still, we move through it like someone could be at home, because you never know.

A cry splits the silence. I stiffen in fear. I wonder what is happening. It came from upstairs.

Jake whispers for us to be quiet. It sounded like a baby.

31

Jake starts up the stairway as silent as a ghost. I will myself to be as quiet as possible. I hear the stairs creaking behind me, letting me know who is right behind me. I assume Leslie is trailing Donna.

We finally reach the top of the stairs. I take shallow breaths, careful to avoid making even the slightest noise. I wish Donna didn't sound like an elephant right about now. Whoever is up there has surely heard all the creaking by now.

Jake steps up to one of the rooms and shines the flashlight around it. Nothing. There are two more doors up here. I stay put, frozen in fear. If that was a baby, then there will likely be a mother or father or both out to protect it. The last thing I want is to get my head blown off.

Jake motions for me to step aside to let Donna and Leslie through. I gladly let them pass by. At least Donna's footsteps aren't as noisy up here. I guess the floor is in better condition up here.

Leslie gives me a nervous glance as she passes me. Since all three of them are dressed like agents, they'll surely come across as more authoritative than me. But then again, being dressed like agents could invite instant gunfire, or worse. I decide to act fast.

"Jake," I say. He doesn't hear me. I'll have to speak louder. "Jake." He turns on me with a hard look.

I sigh. "Look, I was just thinking, if you all barge into a room with a little baby, you're liable to have serious problems. Since none of you are dressed like ordinary people, I think you should let me go first."

I can see the wheels behind Jake's eyes turning as he considers this.

Finally, he says "you're right."

I can't help but feel proud of myself for speaking up when I was so scared. I say, "Hand me the flashlight." And he does.

I step up to one of the doors and gently knock on it. Then, I turn the knob and push until a small gap opens up. "Excuse me, but I heard a baby crying earlier, so I was wondering if something was wrong. My name is Kevin. I am with a small group of people looking for anyone who can give us some useful information. We mean no harm."

"Come in," says a gentle voice. I jerk with a start.

I push the door open until I can finally see the contents of the room. I shine the light around until I find a woman holding a baby in the corner of the room. She is pointing a pistol right at me.

I raise my hands in the air. "It's alright; I'm not one of them. I'm not an agent."

The woman appears to be about twenty-five or thirty years old, and very frightened. She lowers the pistol slowly, prompting me to move a little closer.

"It's alright," I say. "I'm with a group of three other people. Like I said, we're just trying to find someone who knows anything about Garbor, or any of the strange things that's been going on.

I stare at the baby. It is wrapped in a blanket and held tightly in its mother's arms. It's strange seeing a baby. I mean, considering that the Rapture has happened and all, I never thought about babies being left behind.

"Stop right there," says the mother. I come to a stop, not even aware that I was still moving.

"Uh, sorry," I say. I turn around. "My friends are just out in the hallway. They are dressed like agents, though they are just as sane as I am. Honestly, we mean no harm."

"What are you doing here," says the mother. "I mean, with all the agents moving about like fleas on a dog, why did you decide to stop here?"

I take a deep breath. "Because, we noticed that there weren't any lights on, so we assumed the house was vacant. If you don't mind me asking, what are you and your baby doing here?"

The woman laughs. I can see now that she has long dark hair and dark eyes. From this view, she doesn't look a day over twenty.

I breathe a sigh of relief as she lowers the pistol. I swallow hard. I'm just glad that she didn't shoot me.

"Doomsday," says the mother. "That is what you can call the times we are living in. Satan is running wild with no one to stop him. For seven years it's supposed to be like this. As for my baby, well, he was born a couple days ago. He has no idea what the world he lives in is like."

I feel a light bulb turn on in my mind as everything begins to come together. "Oh, that explains why he wasn't Raptured out then because he wasn't born yet. I never thought about what would happen to the babies born after the Rapture. Pardon me, but who helped you deliver it?"

"My best friend, Gracie," she says. "But she has since been picked up. I heard her screams ring out last night as an agent met up with her. My baby and I are alone. This really is hell on earth."

I shiver. "I wonder..." I meet the mother's eyes. "I was just wondering if all that stuff mentioned in Revelation is going to start taking place. You know, where the giant locusts rise out of the earth and sting people. And when the trumpets are sounded, and all the bad stuff starts to happen."

The woman shrugs. "Hard to say, if it will even happen. As for me, I am torn between wanting to believe in the Rapture of the church and an alien abduction. Either way, it is hell on earth."

I shake my head. I don't believe for a minute in an alien abduction. "You know, what with the mark of the beast and everything that's happened recently, I seriously doubt an alien invasion is to blame for everyone's problems."

"She might be right," Leslie says behind me.

I turn around and find myself staring into Leslie's serious eyes. I look at Donna. She looks like she wants to laugh. That's how I feel.

Leslie moves past me, stops a little ways ahead of me. "What's your name?"

The mother looks at her like she is nuts. "That's none of your business."

"Fair enough," Leslie says. "Still, I must say that your theory of an alien invasion seems more realistic than some God beckoning all his people to him in the sky."

The mother laughs. "Well, that's exactly what I was thinking. And, if you watch the news, that is what is being said as well. As for this beast named Vladimir, well, he looks just like anybody else I've ever seen. I don't believe in God anyway."

Leslie turns around and faces Jake. "See what I mean? I'm not the only one out there who thinks sensible thoughts. Just because you believe in God doesn't mean he exists. For example," Leslie says, looking between the three of us, "you all believe that this Vladimir guy is the antichrist when there is no solid evidence to support your claim. It's obvious that someone had to step up to the plate and take over what with all the bad things going on and everything. So, who's to say that anyone was Raptured out period?"

I feel like slapping some sense into Leslie. Instead, I decide to speak. "You know," I say, staring directly at Leslie, "that's just the line of thinking that has kept us out of the Rapture. I use to think the same thing, until I saw people on the news begin to take the mark of the beast. Three sixes tattooed onto your skin should, along with the antichrist, be enough evidence for anyone that we are living in the Great Tribulation."

Leslie looks at me like I've lost it. "The Great Tribulation?" She shakes her head. "I just can't believe that you actually believe this crap. Wouldn't it seem more logical to believe in an alien abduction than the Rapture or Great Tribulation?"

I shake my head. I'm losing patience with her. "No, it wouldn't. Not when all of the Christians are gone. Why would aliens just target Christians and not everyone? Furthermore, your opinion is flawed. If you read the book of Revelation in the Bible, you'd see that what is currently happening is exactly what is mentioned in the book."

Jake lets out an annoyed breath. He looks between Leslie and me. "You know, I don't really care what either of you thinks right now. I just want to get some useful information so that we can find Garbor, the safe haven so that we don't have to face getting our heads chopped off."

I can't help but feel a little agitated at Jake. He makes it sound like my line of thinking is as useless as Leslie's. As it happens, it is information just like this that I have been looking for. Not only is it helpful to know about Garbor, but it is also good to get as much of an idea of what others think as possible. That way, we can better decide for ourselves what has happened. As for me, I have no doubt that the Rapture of the church took place a few months ago. I might not have believed it right off when it made the news, but I think I do now.

I look at the mother. "So what about you? If you don't believe in the Rapture, you probably don't believe in the Bible's mark of the beast either if I'm right."

The mother shakes her head. "You're right, I don't."

I can't help but notice the smirk on her face. "Well, then why don't you go ahead and get the mark so that you'll be able to buy and sell."

"Because" the mother begins, "I don't like the idea of someone telling me what I have to do."

That sounds really stupid. It sounds like she is afraid that the whole mark of the beast thing could be real. I stare at her baby. "You do realize that you're going to need food and supplies for you and your baby. If you don't want to take the mark and you don't want to stay here, why not come with us. We're on our way to Garbor."

"Garbor," says the mother wistfully. She wipes a stray lock of hair out of her eyes.

I nod. "Yeah, but we have a problem. None of us knows how to get there."

The mother laughs. "In that case, I think I'll stay here. Don't really want to take my baby into the wilderness if you know what I mean."

Jake nods. "Fair enough. Now, if you don't mind, could you tell us whether or not you know anyone around here who might be able to help us?"

The mother looks thoughtful. "No, I don't believe I do. Everyone I knew has either disappeared or has taken the mark. That said, you'd be wise to leave this place behind as soon as possible. Servants of Darkness patrol this place fairly regularly now. It'd be unwise to stay too long."

I look at the mother's hands. They are under her baby's blanket. It is almost like she is trying to hide something. I don't like the looks of this.

I stare at her baby. "Can I hold your baby," I say.

The woman pulls further away from me. "No," she says, almost shouting.

I turn to Jake. "Her hands. I think she is hiding something."

Jake narrows his eyes onto me. He turns towards the mother. "Let me see your right hand."

The mother gives him a hard look. "Why should I?"

Jake takes a step towards the mother. "Because I have reason to believe that you are hiding something. And if you are, that means that you are our enemy."

"Fine," the mother says. She waves her right hand in front of Jake. "See, nothing. Now, if you don't mind, I would like to go back to sleep."

Jake gives me a cautious look. Then he turns back to the mother. He walks up to her and motions for her hand.

The woman gives him a hard look. "What is your problem? I already showed you my hand, now leave me alone."

Jake grabs hold of her right hand. He motions for the flashlight. I step out of the way to let Donna pass by.

I have to see this. I move forward until I'm standing on the other side of Donna.

Jake pulls the mother's hand into the light. "There," he says, pointing to the mark. He meets her eyes. "You liar. You're one of them."

The mother starts screaming. Jake lets go of her hand. He looks between Donna and me. I already know what to do, I can see it in his eyes. Jake is the first to leave the room. I follow after him. I can hear Donna and Leslie right on my heels.

I follow Jake out of the house and towards the backyard. I hear Donna scream. I whip around and see her on the ground. She must have tripped.

I rush forward and help Donna to her feet. After a quick thank you, Donna motions for us to continue on after Jake. As for Leslie, I don't see her. She must be with Jake.

I run around the side of the house and into the back yard. I shout for Donna to shine the light to try to find Jake.

"There he is," I say, pointing under a big oak.

I can still hear the mother screaming in the house. She seems content with bringing every agent around down on our heads.

"Jake," I say, coming to a stop in front of him. "What do…"

"No time," Jake says. "We have to leave now."

Jake turns and sets off in the direction we came into the Town. I run beside him, while Donna and Leslie run right behind us.

After several minutes of running, we finally reach the woods. Thank God for the cover.

I rush into the woods right behind Jake. It is all I can do to keep up. It's funny, I always wondered what it would be like if things ever got bad in the country and I had to run to save myself. Now I know that I should have worked out more.

Jake doesn't stop until we reach our supplies. I nearly trip over the log by our supplies as I come to a stop.

"Dang that was close," Jake says.

I nod. Donna, slightly overweight, nods in agreement.

I can imagine the house we left just minutes ago now surrounded by agents. I'm glad we left when we did.

I look around. Oh know, Leslie is nowhere to be seen.

After several minutes of trying to decide what to do, Jake finally decided to head to the edge of the woods to see if he could see any sign of Leslie. I can see him making his way back to us.

Jake shakes his head. "No sign of her. I think they have her."

I feel my heart stop. I have to sit down on the log to keep from passing out. I wipe sweat out of my eyes.

"We need to leave here quickly," Jake says. "If they do have Leslie, they may torture her for information on our whereabouts. If they do, this place could very well be infiltrated by agents in no time."

I shake my head. I look at the ground between my shoes. "I just don't believe it. How...I guess I should have held her hand as we ran from the house."

Jake gives me a sad look, punctuated by impatience. "Don't blame yourself. I took off from the house thinking that all three of you were right behind me. As it is, she may have gotten lost trying to find her way back here. She could actually be fine."

I smile weakly as I detect the disbelief in Jake's voice.

Jake puts a hand on my shoulder. I meet his eyes.

"We have to leave now," he says.

Donna starts gathering the bags as fast as she can. I help her. Now that Leslie is gone, we're all gonna have to carry an extra bag. I wonder if we should maybe leave some of the supplies behind just in case Leslie does finally make it back here. I run this by Jake.

"Okay," he says, sounding hopeful. "Leave two bags behind."

After gathering up our supplies, we head west again. Only this time, instead of almost casual walking, we are on the alert for agents. With all that mother's screaming, it is possible that every agent around is on the lookout for us. I just hope that none of them thinks to check the woods.

I give Jake a sideways glance. "So," I say. "If you don't mind me asking, why didn't you take the mark of the beast? I mean, it would have made your life a lot easier."

Jake snorts a laugh. "Yeah, and doomed me to hell as well. Honestly, I never really believed in the Rapture until a few months ago when everyone suddenly disappeared. It's strange. I always thought I'd have plenty of time to get right with God, but I was wrong and stupid."

I consider what Jake said for a moment. I meet his eyes. "I think the same explanation matches myself. I always thought there'd be enough time to make it right with God. So much for that. And now here I am, right in the middle of hell on earth." I flinch at the word hell.

Donna nods, wipes a stray lock of hair out of her eyes. She meets my eyes. "Then I guess we're all in the same boat. Thing is, I don't know whether Garbor is our best bet after all."

I swallow hard, not liking what she said. "What do you mean?"

"Well," Donna says. "What if there was a place where we could hide out without having to jeopardize our lives. I mean, Garbor surely won't hold out much longer. All it would take would be a big infiltration of agents, and then the Town would fall. Most likely anyways."

Jake looks doubtful. He meets Donna's eyes. "Garbor is said to have a wall over fifty feet high around the entire Town. That would take a great feat to overcome. And then you have the inspections."

"Inspections," I say.

Jake nods. "Yeah, everyone who wants to enter Garbor has to be inspected to make sure that they haven't taken the mark of the beast. Anyone with the mark on their right hand or forehead is denied entrance."

I wonder if Garbor originally began as a Christian settlement. I run this by Jake.

Jake looks contemplative. "I think so. From what I've heard, it began over ten years ago with the intentions of helping people during the Great Tribulation."

Donna adjusts the bags in her hands. She looks between Jake and me. "That's what I heard as well. I also heard that the Town has an underground component."

That sounds cool and safe. "An underground component may be just what we need to escape all the bombing that everyone thinks Garbor is about to receive."

"Yeah," Jake says. "I hear they grow all their food above ground on the compound as well as fish. It's vital that everyone consumes as much protein as possible."

"Fish," I say.

Jake nods. "Yep. Garbor has several well-stocked ponds. Or at least that is what I heard."

Donna looks unconvinced, troubled.

"What is it," I say.

Donna holds a finger to her lips. And then I hear it. Somewhere off in the distance is a loud rumbling sound.

I listen attentively as the steady rumbling makes its way to us. And then it hits.

I look at the ground. I can barely stand up. "It's an earthquake," I say, shouting above the noise.

I try to stay standing as I find myself swaying from side to side. Donna yells beside me, but I couldn't make out what she said.

Donna points to something on the ground ahead of us. It is a long crack in the ground heading our way.

"Run," Jake says.

I drop my bags and take off behind Jake. I saw Donna do the same thing before I took off. I hear her screaming behind me.

"Watch out," Jake shouts, swerving around a dead tree just before it crashes to the ground.

I watch the crack in the ground as I run. It feels like I'm less likely to fall while on the run. I feel like if I just stop for a second, then I'll go crashing down to the ground.

I jump over a log. I don't know which direction we're going. I just know that we're heading away from the large crack that formed on the ground.

We run with no sign of stopping. Although it looks like the crack stopped somewhere behind us, we're still on the run. I'm afraid that if we stop, the crack will catch up with us.

I pray to God to end the earthquake.

And he does.

As soon as the shaking halts, I come to a stop.

"Dang," I say, wiping the sweat out of my eyes. "I thought it had us."

Jake doubles over, taking deep breaths.

Donna looks like she's about to pass out.

I turn around and find a deep crack in the ground behind us. I'm glad I didn't stop a moment sooner, or the ground would have swallowed me up.

I walk to the edge of the crack and look down into it. I can't see the bottom. It is too dark.

Jake steps up beside me, puts a hand on my shoulder. He looks into the crack, careful not to fall in.

"I don't believe it," Jake says. "That was the biggest earthquake I ever experienced. Or ever heard of for that matter."

I nod. "Yeah, I've never seen anything like it. Hey, doesn't it say in the Bible that there will be earthquakes in the last days?"

Jake lets go of my shoulder, looking addled. "Yeah, I think it does."

"Of course it does," Donna says, but not unkindly. "And if I'm right, there's also supposed to be severe drought, terrible sores, and darkness that you can feel. My guess is that was just a small earthquake."

I swallow hard. We barely got away with our lives. I wish so much that I had been ready for the Rapture of the church.

I back away from the crack in the ground. I look at Jake. "So much for all our food and supplies."

Jake wipes sweat out of his dark eyes. "Just be glad we got away with our lives."

I nod.

Donna steps up to the crack and looks inside of it. "I wonder how deep it is."

Jake shrugs. "Hard to say, but as bad as it sounds, it may have helped us."

I look at Jake like he's nuts. "In what way," I say.

Jake nods at the crack. "I'd say it made those agents forget all about us. And if they have, we'll be a lot safer."

"Yeah," Donna says, backing away from the crack. "I guess it took something big to stop them from getting to us."

I guess Donna's right. I bet they would have put dogs on us if it hadn't been for that earthquake. Now they've probably got other things to think about.

I look at the trees. I'm surprised that most of them are still standing. I wonder what the earthquake did to the Towns.

"Probably leveled the Towns," Jake says, as though he read my mind.

"You really think so," I say.

Jake shakes his head from side to side. "Well, there's a good chance it did, but maybe it didn't. I bet it didn't do them any good."

I turn to Donna. She still looks shaken. I can tell that like me, she is also aggravated that we had to leave our food and other supplies behind. There's no way we could have ran like we did if we had to hold two or three heavy bags full of stuff.

I lower myself to the ground. I don't think I could stand another moment. My legs are killing me.

Donna sits beside me, followed by Jake.

We sit for several minutes just staring into the huge crack in front of us. I wonder why God stopped the earthquake when he did. Surely it wasn't to protect us. I run this by Jake and Donna.

Donna fidgets her fingers. "Don't know. I always thought that God was too important to have much to do with small folk like us. But then again, I've been wrong before."

"I think he did," Jake says. "Stop the ground from eating us, I mean. You know," Jake says, looking at me, "it makes sense. Since none of us have taken the mark of the beast, perhaps God thinks that there is still hope for us. As for myself, I know there is."

I try thinking back to some Bible verses that I read many years ago. Unfortunately, none of them are coming to mind right now.

"It's funny," Donna says, tossing broken sticks into the crack. "If there is a God, and I think there is, he could have taken us out if that crack had been moving just a little bit faster. It's like he stopped it just before it consumed us. Seems like something similar happened thousands of years ago back in Biblical times when the ground opened up and swallowed some people."

I feel taken aback. "It did," I say.

Donna nods. "Yep, and it only happened to the people who had sinned against God. God won't let things touch you if you are His child. He takes care of those who are His."

I sigh. I stare at the crack. "I wonder what kinds of stuff we're going to experience before Jesus comes back for the second time." I give Donna a sideways glance. "I know what all you said is supposed to happen, but we might not be alive for all of it."

Jake looks thoughtful. "It's hard to say, but I don't think Jesus cares a great deal about us at any rate."

I frown. "What do you mean?"

Jake shrugs. "Well, take all these end times disasters for instance. If God really cared much about us, he wouldn't be subjecting us to such terrible things. I think God is more concerned about keeping His word than He is about relieving our suffering."

I shake my head. "I don't think so. According to the Bible, or at least what I can remember of it, God is a loving God. He isn't punishing us for no reason. He's punishing us because we failed to accept Jesus Christ as our Lord and Savior. That's why we're here, and everyone else is in heaven."

"And probably eating a lot better too," Donna says. "You know, the Bible talks about the marriage supper of the Lamb that's supposed to occur sometime during the Great Tribulation. Unfortunately, people like us who missed the Rapture won't be in on the feast."

I laugh. Donna gives me a funny look. I shrug. "Well, you have to admit that it is kind of funny. I mean, here we are down here with all hell breaking loose, and everyone else is up there eating high on the hog."

Donna laughs. "Yeah, it is kind of strange."

Jake sighs, throws a stick into the crack. "I just hope we're right."

I can't help but look a little startled. "What do you mean?"

"What if there isn't a God," Jake says. "I mean, what if what we thought was the Rapture of the church was an alien abduction or something. If so, that would mean that the Rapture hasn't happened yet, if it will ever happen."

I look at Jake's hands in his lap. "So what's keeping you from taking the mark of the beast, other than the part where you'll lose your soul, of course?"

Jake bites down onto his lower lip. "I don't know. I guess a greater part of me believes in God and the Bible, it's just not the most sensible part of me right now."

"Yeah," Donna says, tying her shoestrings. "I think I'm somewhere between wanting to believe in God and actually believing in Him if that makes any sense."

I nod. "It does. I just hope that you two can figure it out before much longer. It's too dangerous nowadays to not know exactly where you stand on these issues. If we all believed like we were supposed to, none of us would be here right now. As for an alien abduction, that was what the antichrist came up with, wasn't it?"

Donna nods. "I think so. At least that's what he said on the news. And speaking of the antichrist, there's something interesting about him that makes me think he could possibly be the Messiah."

I feel my jaw drop. "Donna. How could you say that? The antichrist is supposed to mimic God so that everyone left on earth will follow him." I put my hands on the ground and turn my body to face Donna. "And furthermore, he wants everyone to take his mark so that they will lose their souls while following him. So," I say, hardly believing that I have to say this, "Vladimir, the antichrist I mean, wants everyone to be fooled by him. I wouldn't be one bit surprised if he requires people to use capital letters when addressing him as the supreme ruler of the universe."

"But what if he really is God," Jake says.

I turn around to face Jake. I feel light headed. These two are worse off than me, and that's bad. "That's exactly what the antichrist wants you to think. He wants you to worship him and lose your soul in the process. He wants you to believe in God, himself that is, so he can deceive you. But here's the bad thing: If you don't believe in the right God, you can still lose your soul. Isn't that what Satan came to do, to kill, steal, and destroy?"

Jake looks unconvinced. "Maybe so, but there's no real way of knowing whether this Vladimir is really the antichrist or Jesus Christ."

You have got to be kidding. "If he was Jesus Christ, he'd say so. All he has said so far is that he is for everyone taking his mark. But there's something else to consider: It says in the Bible that the antichrist would come bearing the special number of six six six. It all comes down to the fact of whether or not you believe the Bible. With everything going on around us these days, I do."

"That's a good point," Donna says behind me. I turn around to face her. She looks like she actually believes what I said, compared to Jake's wishy washy perspective. "If it said in the Bible that the antichrist's number was six six six, then I believe it. My mother used to talk about the Bible all the time, and she was one of the ones who went missing. Surely the Rapture has occurred."

Jake looks at us like we're both nuts. "I don't believe it. If you two believe that crap in the Bible, then you'd be susceptible to believing anything. As for me, I think there's more to the picture than any of us knows."

"Like what," I say, losing my patience.

"Like one plus one is still two," Jake says. I can't help but feel like this is the first time he has ever come across like a smart aleck. Jake looks slightly apologetic. "Look, I just think there's more that happened than we're aware of, that's all."

I don't know what to do, whether to shrug it off or nod in agreement. Instead, I just sit quietly. I don't think he'd believe much of what I said right now anyway.

After what feels like two or three hours of sitting here, Jake finally rises to his feet.

"What is it," I say.

Jake taps his watch. "It's a good time to travel now, in the dark. Well, it's not completely dark, at least we have the moon on our side."

I look up at the moon. "For now anyway."

CHAPTER 3 The Capture

Donna nods. "Yeah, it wouldn't surprise me one bit if it didn't just go completely black all at once."

I glance at the ground. I sure wouldn't want to be walking around this crack if it happened.

We set off, side by side into the night. I hear an owl hooting off in the distance. A few seconds later another owl responds to the first one. I laugh inwardly.

I wish we had something to eat. I wish we didn't have to leave all our stuff behind. But it was either that or face certain death.

"You know," I say, glancing at Jake and Donna, "if we could just find an old run down shed I'll be a happy camper."

"Same here," Donna says. "I'm tired, hungry, worried, and miserable. I don't know what it is, but ever since the Rapture of the church, I haven't been as comfortable. It's like my mind is telling me that I've missed my chance and now I have to be uncomfortable."

I laugh. "Yeah, I know the feeling. I think that's because the spirit of God is no longer on the earth or something."

"Really," Jake says. "I think it would be wiser to attribute our misery to the fact that we've been on the run without hardly any proper rest. That's enough to make anybody miserable."

"It's probably a combination," Donna says.

I nod.

And then it dawns on me. We had to leave our flashlight behind. Man. I was hoping that we could have held on to that for as long as possible. I run this by Jake and Donna.

"Yeah," Jake says. "Tough luck."

Donna nods sadly.

I stare at the top of the map sticking out of Jake's pocket. "So where to now?"

Jake looks at me like I should know the answer to that question. "West, of course. I hope we can find someone like us who haven't yet taken the mark. We need information badly. And since the map lacks much of the detail we need, we're going to have to rely on people for the lion's share of our information."

I nod. "I wish that woman hadn't led us on. Why do you think she did that?"

"The mother you mean," Jake says, glancing at me. I nod. "Probably because she was scared. By acting like she hadn't yet taken the mark, she was also protecting her baby."

I frown. "What?"

Jake sighs. "I mean that she was using the lack of the mark as a tool to protect her baby. I doubt her baby had the mark of the beast."

Strange. I've never thought of a baby having the mark of the beast before. Since babies don't buy and sell, I guess that's why it never occurred to me. I meet Jake's eyes nonetheless. "So, you're saying that she was protecting her baby by leading us on."

Jake nods. "Exactly."

"She probably thought we'd turn her in or something," Donna says. "As strange as it may seem, a baby without the mark could be a dangerous discovery. I heard on the news several weeks ago that even babies were expected to take the mark of the beast. I think they called it the Baby's Mark."

I didn't know that. "So that's why she was leading us on. She didn't want her baby's lack of mark to be discovered. Thing is, we never paid any attention to the baby, did we?"

Donna nods. "I did. And he or she didn't have the mark on its hand or head. But I don't think babies can lose their souls even if they are marked."

"Good point," I say. "It's not like they can help it. But at least we know now why the mother was acting so strange."

My stomach growls. I look at Jake. "When do you think we're going to be able to eat something?"

Jake shrugs. "Difficult to say, but probably not too much longer. Even if I have to break in a house and confiscate food with my fake ID, we are going to eat. We also need to think about finding you an agent's uniform."

I frown miserably. Just what I wanted to hear. The last thing I want is to have to wear an agent's uniform. Nevertheless, I can understand

Jake's reasoning. "So where do you think we're going to find a properly sized uniform?"

Jake pats his pistol. "I could always threaten one of them. The thing is, he'd have to be about your size to make all the trouble worthwhile."

Donna looks me over. "You have a build like most agents have, so you shouldn't have any problem with procuring a uniform. But I have to tell you, they stink. And I'm not talking about an odor. If our success weren't so dependent on our dress, I'd tear these rags off in a heartbeat. As it is, I need to stop somewhere and wash and brush and get a drink."

I lean into Donna and sniff. "Yeah, you do smell kind of unpleasant. What'd you do, wallow in Servants of Darkness fragrance?"

Donna laughs. "It sure seems like it. The woman who I got my uniform off of was wearing some kind of flowery perfume, so your theory isn't far off."

Jake comes to a stop. He motions for Donna and I to stop talking. So we do.

"Listen," Jake says, directing his ear to a sound.

I turn my ear in the same direction and listen. I hear a low growl, like an engine or something. And then it fades away.

I look at Jake. "What do you think that was?"

"Probably a tank or something," Jake says. "It's difficult to say, but it didn't sound like any car or truck I ever heard of."

"Me either," Donna says. "In fact, the last time I heard something like that, the Town where I'm from was being invaded by Agents of Darkness."

"Really," I say.

Donna nods. "It was late in the day when they came, but they came nonetheless. I was sitting outside shelling peas on the front porch when I heard them. And then I saw them. First, they'd ask everyone to surrender to the beast, the antichrist that is, and then take his mark. Anyone that refused was arrested and taken prisoner. The houses of those who refused to take the mark were bulldozed away."

"That's terrible," I say, earning a nod from Donna. "That's not how it happened where I'm from. In my Town, the agents came waltzing in with rifles and tear gas. I left as soon as I figured out what was going on. If I had stayed, I would have been forced to take the mark of the beast or die. At least that is what I heard was happening from the Towns in other districts. And since I was living in an apartment, I had few possessions. Apart from my father's watch, there was nothing else valuable enough for me to take."

"Interesting," Donna says.

Jake looks like he remembered something. "Oh, about that watch," he says, reaching into his pocket. He takes it out and hands it to me. "Here, before I forget and trade it for something we need."

I take it and shove it into my pocket. "Thanks," I say, feeling some better.

I want to tell Jake that he reminds me of the older brother I never had, but I decide not to. I don't want him to feel like I trust him completely just yet.

After handing me the watch, Jake sets off towards the area where he heard the tanks. Fortunately, it is to the west. Donna and I fall into step beside him.

"What are you expecting to find," I say to Jake.

Jake's dark eyes scan my face. "Someone or something useful I hope. If the former, then we'd better be prepared to do some witty talking. If the latter, then we won't be any worse off than we are now."

I hope he's right.

As we move further in the direction of the tanks, I begin to hear people talking. Jake tells Donna and me to hunker down and stay alert. I wish I was wearing an agent's uniform. I would just feel better right now.

"Look," whispers Jake, pointing to a group of people. They're standing around several tanks. "If we could get one of those tanks, then we'd be in business."

I want to laugh.

"You know," Donna says to Jake, "since you have senior agent registration, you could just waltz right up there and figure out what's going on."

Jake frowns, looks like he wants to say something sharp to Donna but decides against it. Instead, he says "We'll wait until nightfall, then we'll head in. If we go in now, it will look too suspicious. They'd want to know where we came from and why we just appeared so suddenly."

Jake backtracks a short distance to a safer place. Then, he sits down on a fallen log. I gladly sit on one side of him while Donna sits at his other side. And now we wait.

I watch as the sun sets, quickly plunging the wooded area into darkness. If we can find our way to the agent's camp, I'll be surprised. My luck I'd head in the opposite direction when we need to head west.

Once the last of the orange hue leaves the horizon, Jake rises to his feet. He looks between Donna and me. "It's time."

I spring to my feet, my stomach accounting for much of my motivation. I am so hungry, and yet we have absolutely nothing to eat. More than information, I'd do about anything to get a meal right about now.

We set out, one behind the other so that we'll be less likely of getting caught. I walk behind Donna, who managed to rush in behind Jake before I could.

Part of me wants to grab a stick for protection, but I'm hoping that it won't come to that. Now that I think of it, it would have probably been a better idea to leave one or two of us behind. Perhaps Jake would have been safer if he had gone alone. I quietly run this by him.

He shakes his head, stops to look at me. "No, because if I get in a tank, I'm not going back. As it is, we have a good chance of getting some form of vehicle tonight, if we use our heads."

Right. I want to tell him that that counts me out just for a laugh but now is not the time.

Like a ghost, Jake sneaks up behind a large tent next to the woods. It looks like a perfect place to pillage. I just hope there is food involved.

Jake turns around to face Donna and me. "Stay here for a moment. If the tent is occupied I'll come back, and we'll go a different direction, but if it isn't then, I'll do some speedy investigating before I come back."

I nod. Donna and I exchange nervous glances. I swallow hard. I sure hope Jake knows what he is doing. Now that I've gotten use to him being around, I'd hate to lose him.

Donna and I decide to sit down while we wait. I think both of us are running pretty low on energy about now.

I look at the area around the tent. I wonder where all the agents went? I don't see hide nor hair of them.

"You know," Donna whispers, leaning into me, "if we could get a tank, or even a car or truck, we could cover so much ground we'd be bound to make it to Garbor sooner than later."

I stifle a laugh. Donna's right. I hope that Jake manages to find out some useful stuff because we need it.

I lean against a tree while I wait for Jake to return. At least I'm sitting down. Even though my stomach isn't satisfied, at least my legs are.

I wish my watch worked. It feels like Jake has been gone for hours. My biggest fear apart from him getting caught is seeing an orange tinge in the sky, signaling the soon to rise sun.

I see a shadow emerge from the darkness. It is Jake. Thank God!

Jake hunkers down in front of us and hands us each something. I squish my fingers over the plastic, trying to figure out what it is.

And then I do. "It's food," I say, hardly believing my ears. It looks like some kind of sandwich.

Jake nods. "Got it from one of the tents. You'd better eat it in a hurry. If I'm right, I think we might be able to get a free ride from this place."

I frown. "What do you mean?"

Jake looks happier than I've ever seen him. "I mean that those guys over there aren't agents, they're just like us. None of them have taken the mark of the beast yet. They're planning a rescue mission, to help people like us escape to Garbor."

At that, I rise to my feet with an inward howl. I suddenly feel stronger, like a hungry wolf. Still, I look at Jake. "You're sure. I mean you didn't see any agents."

"None," Jake says. "The coast is clear. As a matter of fact, some of the guys have asked us to bunk with them for the night."

"Us," Donna says, questioningly.

Jake nods. "Yep, I already told them about us. One of the guys said that they barely escaped that big crack that formed in the ground during the earthquake. Said he heard on the radio that several Towns north of here have been leveled."

"Gosh," I say, trying not to think only about the food I'm holding.

"Well, let's go then," Jake says. He turns around and sets off, straight and tall. Donna and I follow him, eating along the way.

"This sandwich is really good," I say.

Donna nods. "Mine is too."

Jake stops in front of a large tent and points inside of it. "Here is where we'll be staying tonight. If all goes well, we'll be heading out early in the morning. One guy said he would take us to within a hundred miles of Garbor, then he'd have to turn back."

"Wow," I say, hardly believing my ears. "Within a hundred miles?"

Jake nods. "Yep, and he even said he'd supply us with two days worth of food. I figure that we can find someone else at the base where he's taking us to take us the rest of the hundred mile journey."

"Oh that's great," Donna says, clapping her hands together. "We'll be safe there, in Garbor, I mean."

"Is there more of these," I say, holding up an empty wrapper.

Jake smiles. "By the coolers full. And there's also plenty of clean drinking water to boot. I even saw some lemonade, if you can believe that."

I want to throw my hands into the air and shout. This is definitely our night. Who would have thought that we would happen across such a fortune? And, if God had not allowed the earthquake, we probably wouldn't be here right now. I run this by Jake and Donna.

Jake looks convinced. "I'm beginning to believe in that God of yours."

I grin. "He's not just my God," I say. "He's everyone's God. Well, at least he made everyone. Unfortunately, not everyone has accepted Him, and that's why we're here now."

"Yeah," Jake says. "I guess so."

"Hey, I say, pointing at Jake. He looks wild eyed. "I bet we can get loads of information here. I bet these guys know exactly what all's been going on in the country."

"Probably," Jake says. "I mean if they don't then who would?"

Donna points an index finger into the sky. "Thank you, Jesus. I knew you'd provide a way of escape for me, for us, I mean."

"Follow me," Jake says. "There's someone I want you to meet."

I follow along gladly. We pass by several smaller tents as well as groups of tanks and other vehicles. I eye the vehicles wistfully.

Jake comes to a stop. I almost run into him. He turns and faces Donna and me. He points at a man wearing a dark shirt and a cap. "This is Frederick," he says. "Frederick, this is Donna and Kevin."

I extend a hand to Frederick. He shakes it instantly, which makes me happy. I always hated being the first one to break the ice, but sometimes, it's not so bad.

Frederick points to the sandwich in Donna's hand. "There's plenty more of them where that came from. And from the looks of you all, you need 'em."

I poke the empty plastic wrap from my sandwich into my pocket. Then, I meet Frederick's eyes. "So you're really unmarked?"

Frederick nods.

"That's awesome," I say. "Ever since I've been on the run, I've thought that we three were among the very few unmarked."

Frederick laughs. "Yeah, I can see how you'd think that. You know, where I come from, hardly anyone took the mark. Over half of them's dead now mind you."

I feel sad about that.

"So what about this rescue mission," Donna says. "Where will you head next?"

"Away from that crack left behind from that earthquake for starters," Frederick says. "Then, wherever anyone exists who needs rescuing. I ain't got no preference really, just want to help all the folks we can."

"That's great," I say.

Frederick motions to a table and chairs a few yards away. "Might as well be sitting than standing."

I agree. And my legs have stood about all they're going to for the day. That run from the earthquake crack about did me in.

I sit in a chair across from Frederick. Jake sits on one side of me while Donna sits on my other side.

"So," Jake says, looking at Frederick. "We need information. If you could tell us anything about Garbor, or what's going on in the other districts, we'd really appreciate it."

"Sure," Frederick says, gently tugging at his beard. "Well, I guess what we do here is a good place to start off. There are exactly forty-eight of us at this campsite along. There are other campsites that have even more unmarked. As for us, we just figure that there's unmarked in just about every Town, so we just move from Town to Town helping anyone who looks like they could use some help."

"What about the agents," Jake says. "How much of a presence do they have around here?"

Frederick looks serious. "Not very many around these parts. Agents mainly stay in the Towns. So, you all have done right to avoid the highways and Towns. And speakin of agents," he says looking at Jake, "you sure had me fooled at first. I was fixin to beat the daylights out of you before you spoke up."

Jake lets out a nervous laugh.

"What about Garbor," Donna says. "What can you tell us about that?"

Frederick clasps his hands on the table. "Well for starters, I know it's where people like us can go for safety. I got a couple of friends who are there now. Amos and Tiggs their names. I helped 'em get over halfway there before I was told by my boss to turn around and head back to help deal with an emergency."

"What kind of an emergency," I say.

"Top secret," Frederick says. "Can't tell you that. But I can tell you that Garbor is everything you've heard it is. It's full of good people, the unmarked mostly."

I frown. "What do you mean, mostly?"

Frederick looks at me kind of funny, like I should already know this. "Not everyone in Garbor is unmarked. Some of the people there have taken the mark of the beast."

"No," Donna says, looking absolutely horrified.

Frederick nods. "Yep, and knows they made a big mistake to. I suppose they've been paying attention to all the signs and everything, though some of the marked are just hoping that they can have the tattooed removed so that they can go to heaven. Can't go to heaven with the mark of the beast, and they know it."

I feel my jaw drop. I never thought about that, about getting the mark removed after you've taken it.

"And most of 'ems good folks," Frederick says. "Speaking of the marked I mean. There's a lot of them who are just good folks who made bad choices. But then again, I reckon there are plenty of good folks in hell right about now."

I feel light headed. I wish I had something to drink. I want to ask for something, but I'm too invested in the information coming out of Frederick's mouth.

"But back to Garbor," Frederick says, "some of 'em that I've talked to said that it's the best Town of refuge that exists."

Jake leans into the table. "What do you mean some of them?"

Frederick considers this. "Well, I reckon because there are a few of 'em here tonight. I'll introduce you to a few of them tomorrow morning before we head out."

Jake nods. "Sounds good."

After several more minutes of chatting, Frederick leads us to one of the nearest tents, where we will be spending the night. It looks comfortable. I take a cot towards the back of the tent, while Jake and Donna are in the middle. I feel a lot safer this far away from the entrance.

That night, I dream about agents swooping in on us and arresting us. Then, we are put on a bus and shipped to the nearest headquarters. I am told that I can either take the mark of the beast or lose my life. Or, as one of the agents put it, he can tattoo me with the mark of the beast whether I want it or not. The thing is, if someone marks you without your consent, does that still mean that you can lose your soul? I mean, as long as you've got the mark, it looks like the worst case scenario for you.

"Move," says a voice. "They're heading this way."

In my mind, I move to the side to let the people pass by. I hear fireworks somewhere off in the distance. I rise from my bed and look out the window. The night sky is decorated with all different colors. A giant cobra rises up in the sky and strikes at me. I jump backward.

"Get up," says a familiar voice. I turn around and face my bedroom door. It sounds like someone is standing just outside my door. "Come on, wake up."

I wake to a punch in the arm. I give Jake an indignant look.

Jake looks apologetic, but also upset. "There are agents swooping in on us, we need to go now."

I nod. I scramble to my feet.

"Here," Donna says, motioning at my shoes. "Let me help you. We don't have much time."

"Thanks," I say, suddenly realizing the seriousness of the situation.

"There," Donna says. "Now let's go."

I follow Jake and Donna out of the tent and into the night. Loud voices pierce the air around me, making me feel a little dizzy.

Jake leads us across the camp, around several other tents, and towards a densely wooded area.

I blink and Jake and Donna are gone. I enter the woods behind them.

"Hey," I say, not able to see either of them. "Wait up."

"Come on," says a voice from just up ahead. "This way. Follow my voice."

Someone takes hold of my arm, stopping me. I try to jerk my arm away, but can't. The hold is just too tight.

"Be still," Jake says. "That was an agent who just called to you."

I search the area for any sign of Donna but don't see her. My heart sinks. She must have gotten lost or caught.

Screaming fills the heavy air around us. It sounds like Donna.

I look at Jake. "We have to help her."

Jake shakes his head. "It's too dangerous."

I feel my jaw drop. "She is part of this group, or haven't you noticed?"

Jake looks unyielding. "Be quiet."

I jerk my arm out of his grasp. I want to punch him in the arm like he did to me, but decide it best to control my anger.

Light suddenly fills the air around us.

"Get down," Jake says, pulling me to the ground with him. "And be quiet."

I watch in fear as someone holding a flashlight pans the area around us. I pray to God that we go unnoticed.

Slowly, the person holding the flashlight moves steadily away from us. I breathe a sigh of relief.

I hope Donna's alright. I wonder what happened to her.

"Okay," Jake says. "I think we can move now."

I watch as Jake slowly rises to his feet. I follow suit. After telling me to follow him, he moves from tree to tree, trying to avoid being seen.

I hear screaming and gun shots at the camp behind us. I half consider telling Jake to go back and look for Donna, but it is just too dangerous. Thing is, I could have sworn I seen her follow Jake into the woods. I guess she just got lost. Or she got caught by an agent.

I continue following Jake into the unknown. I'm trying to stay as close to him as possible. The last thing I want is to get lost. I'm not even sure which direction we're heading anymore. I guess it doesn't matter that much as long as we get as far away from camp as possible.

Jake comes to a stop. He takes something out of his pocket. I squint my eyes to try to see what it is. It looks like a box of matches. He lights a match and then holds it next to a compass.

"There," he says, looking at the compass. "We were heading east."

Well, at least we're heading in the right direction now. I didn't know that Jake had a compass. Honestly, he could have told me.

Jake puts the compass and box of matches back into his pocket. Then he meets my eyes. He shakes his head like he just can't believe what happened.

"We need to head back," he says, shocking me. "I know we shouldn't, but we need to see what happened to Donna. Since I am dressed like an agent and have a registration card, I think I can do it. Worst case scenario, I'll be caught."

I swallow hard. "But I don't want to be left here while you backtrack. I mean, who knows if you'd ever find me again."

"Good point," Jake says. "That's why you're coming with me at least part of the way. I'll leave you in the woods just outside of camp. That way, if something happens and I don't come back, you'll have an idea where you are. Oh, and here," Jake says, reaching into his pockets. He hands me the compass. "Just in case I don't come back, you'll need it."

I nod. With that said, Jake turns around and heads back to the camp. The strange thing is, I don't hear any of the noise that I heard earlier. We're either too far away from camp to hear it, or it has all settled down.

"Now," Jake begins, "chances are, everyone is still in their safe places if there are still agents around. So, since I'm dressed like an agent, I'm going to have to be extremely careful not to get shot. I plan on trying to find Frederick, but I may not be able to. We will have to wait and see."

I have a bad feeling about this. "Maybe we should wait, until morning that is. We could use the light to help us."

Jake shakes his head. "No, I need to go in now. I need to see whether or not Donna has been captured. If she has, then I plan on breaking her out."

That sounds like a nearly impossible job. I run this by him.

"We'll have to wait and see," he says. "But I can tell by your expression that you think it's a lost cause if Donna's been captured. The thing is, I've known Donna for several years. I was the one who asked her to come with me, so I feel a little responsible."

We finally make it to the edge of the woods. Everything is strangely quiet. It looks like everyone has left. I can't tell if there are any tanks or other vehicles still there or not.

I nod at Jake's pistol. "Don't forget about that. If you have to use it, better them than you."

Jake nods. "Yeah, but don't worry too much. I can't shirk the feeling that something went on here out of the ordinary."

I frown. "Meaning?"

Jake swallows hard. "Meaning that for some reason, the tents are all still intact and yet there isn't a person around to be seen. I mean, it looks like the agents would have at least stuck around and investigated the camp. But from what I can tell, everything is right where it was when we left. That said, I'm anxious to try to figure out what happened. We've only been gone a little over a half hour, so it looks like there'd still be people milling about, but there's not."

I look at the camp. "Maybe it's a trap."

"Could be," Jake says. "But I intend to figure out what happened here tonight. You wait here while I go out and investigate. If I don't come back within a reasonable amount of time, then you get yourself as far away from here as you can. And don't forget to use that compass."

I nod. And with that, Jake steps into the open. I lean against the tree, my eyes scanning the camp. Jake was right. I don't see any sign of anyone.

Minutes roll by, but still no sign of Jake. I half considered going in, but I'm afraid to do so in case there are hidden agents. And since I don't have a uniform like Jake, I'd have a tuff time trying to convince anyone that I am an agent.

I feel a drop of sweat run down my back. I wish I knew what went on here tonight. From the looks of it, Jake will not be coming back anytime soon. As a matter of fact, I don't see any sign of him. It looks like he would have at least come back by now and let me know what he has discovered. As it is, I'm left here to dream up the worst case scenario. If he has been captured, then there is nothing I can do for him. I'll just have to leave and see if I can make it to Garbor on my own. I just can't believe that I practically started out with three other companions, only to be left alone here and now.

I listen closely for any possible sound. Nothing. Nor is there any campfires glowing orange like there was when we left. It is as if someone wanted to make it difficult to see anyone period. I wish I could run this by Jake, but it is too late. Or is it? The thing is, if Jake had gotten into any trouble, it looks like he would have yelled or something. Or would he? I don't know him that well to make an educated guess. Before recently, I didn't even know he existed.

I scan the camp one last time. I better go. I don't like the looks of this place one bit. At this point, there is nothing I can do to help Jake. Nor would he want me to put myself in danger just to try to find him. So, with that said, I think it is time to head out.

I turn around and come face to face with an unknown.

Before I can say anything, the man slaps a hand over my mouth. I try to pry his fingers off, but can't, he is just too strong.

"Stay quiet," he says, slowly removing his hand from my mouth.

Now I see who he is. "Frederick," I say, frowning. "What are you doing here?"

"I told you to stay quiet," he barks.

I nod, beginning to understand.

Frederick motions for me to turn around and face camp. So I do.

I see someone exit one of the nearest tents, the first person I've seen since we've come back. I watch in anxiety as the person disappears into the darkness.

I turn around and face Frederick. I know I'll have to whisper. "Who was that? What's going on?"

Frederick looks shaken to the core. "Agents, dozens of them. I hate to say this, but both of your friends Jake and Donna have been arrested. As far as I could tell, I was the only unmarked that made it out undetected."

"What," I say, sounding far off.

Frederick gives me a half worried, half sad look. "We need to follow them. From what I can tell, most of the agents have left the premises. I saw your friend Jake get arrested just a couple of minutes before I found you. I figured he left you here, so I decided to investigate where I saw him leave the woods behind."

I swallow hard. "Thanks." I'm at a loss of words. I can't believe Jake has been arrested. I guess I figured that his uniform and fake ID would have saved him.

"What about Donna," I say. "How do you know for sure she was arrested?"

"Because" Frederick begins, "I was there when it happened. She tripped over a log right after she ran into the woods, and then several agents swooped down on her before she had time to get up. I was hiding behind a bush when it happened. There was nothing I could do. I'm sorry."

I want to beat my head against a wall. I can't believe this has happened. Jake and I would have been better off if we had never come back if we had just forgotten about Donna. I run this by Frederick.

Frederick shakes his head from side to side. "I can understand Jake wanting to see what happened to her. They were good friends, that much was apparent. I just wish that I had found him sooner before the agents did."

"So what now," I say, scanning the camp for any movement. "I mean, if there are still agents out there, what should we do?"

"I'm staying until tomorrow morning," Frederick says. "Got to avoid getting caught by an agent. It's too risky to try to prowl around in the dark."

I nod. "Yeah, I guess it would be. Do you know if there are any vehicles left?"

Frederick nods. "From what I could tell, they were all still there. The thing is, you can't see them from here. I reckon the agents will come back for everything valuable in time. I just hope we can get a van before they do."

"A van," I say, feeling a little stupid.

"Yes," Frederick says. "There are four vans, six tanks, and two cars. But unlike the other vehicles, the vans are filled with food and other supplies that we need. That's why I want one of them. They also have gas cans in them so we can make it a lot farther."

I nod. "Sounds good." I can't help but frown. "Where do you plan on going?"

Fredrick gives me a firm look. "To Garbor. If we can make it there, then we'll have it made. If not, well, God help us."

I swallow hard.

Frederick hunkers down and motions for me to follow suit, so I do. I squint my eyes and see a dark figure walking in front of one of the tents. It must be an agent. It's strange how your eyes can adapt to darkness, allowing you to see some things.

I try to breathe as shallowly as possible in order to go unnoticed.

Before long, I can feel myself drifting off to sleep. Frederick is now laying on his back, the edge of his shoes at the edge of a big bush. I'm thankful that the bush is providing us some good cover.

I decide to lay down as well. Next thing I know, I see a huge building with big white columns out in the middle of nowhere. I look at the time on my watch to see what time the antichrist is supposed to speak. Only two more minutes. I can't believe I'm actually here, that I'm actually this close to the greatest threat on the earth.

Finally, Vladimir steps out onto the porch and positions himself in front of the podium. "Welcome friends," he says, in a gentle voice. You'd think he was harmless. "I'm sorry to keep you waiting. I do have a very important announcement to make. Just last night, on the other side of Wertenland, two people were captured and brought here to my special quarters. It appears that both of these people were dressed as agents and were attempting to make it to Garbor. But, fortunately for them, they have both decided to take my mark. So, as I stand here before you, I want you to give a round of applause to two of our newest members of the dark brotherhood. Please welcome Jake Schimper and Donna Zeeland."

Thousands upon thousands of people suddenly appear in front of the white columned building. I can hear them chanting the name of the antichrist, as well as chanting "life to the dead, may they come alive."

Vladimir raises a hand, causing the mass of people to go silent. "I have other news that I'm sure will delight you. Just last night, I had the opportunity to speak to the group of lesser rulers in this New World Order. They have all agreed to give me omnipotent power in order to safeguard our kingdom from any foes that might arise. And on a happy

61

note, I would now like to make a formal blasphemy against the God of heaven, who I'm afraid still believes himself to be more powerful than I. So," Vladimir says, looking towards the heavens, "by the power vested in me, I curse you, God of Israel, ruler of nothing. I also curse his angels, who have much less power than me, for it was I who was shot and came back to life. It is I who am the Son of the most high God. Without me, this world would have no God to look to. Moreover, I am pleased to announce that all new members to our brotherhood will become priests to serve in my temples. Thank you and good night."

I swallow hard. So Jake and Donna have decided to take the mark of the beast. I just can't believe it. How did they get to the Capitol so soon? I guess they must have ridden on one of the new airplanes. I still can't believe it. Now Jake and Donna will lose their souls. I would much rather lose my head than my soul.

I watch as the thousands of people gathered in front of the Capitol building begin to disperse. It looks like one of the biggest gatherings that I have ever seen. I wonder…

"Wake up," says a voice. Someone shakes my shoulder. "It's time to go."

I open my eyes to an impatient Frederick standing over me. I rub the sleep from my eyes and breathe a sigh of relief that it was just a dream.

I rise to my feet cautiously.

Frederick nods at the camp, now apparently free of agents. "I already had a look. There are no agents anywhere to be seen. The bad thing is, all of the vehicles have been taken. So, we'll have to go on foot, at least for a while."

Great, just what I wanted to hear. I can't help but let out an annoyed sigh. I was really looking forward to being transported across country instead of having to walk. All well, I guess God doesn't want things to be easy on me, what with me being left behind and all.

Frederick meets my eyes with a cautious look. "Let's go. If we have any luck, we might run into some of my kind down the road. There were several groups of us. It just so happened that my group decided to stay here for a while."

I nod. That would be good.

I follow Frederick out of the woods and into the camp. He leads me towards one of the biggest tents in the area.

"They'll probably send someone here to take the tents," Frederick says impatiently. "But, before they do, I intend to get all the supplies we'll need. And hopefully enough to last us a few days."

I walk into the tent behind Frederick. He seems to know where he is going. If everything had gone as planned, we would have been leaving this morning for Garbor. But that's life. It always has a way of giving you the unexpected.

Frederick motions me forward. "Here," he says, handing me a duffel bag. "Try to cram as much food and water as you can into them. You also might look around for other things including matches, blankets, and anything else that we could use."

I nod.

Within a short time, my duffel bag gets stuffed with so much that there is no longer any room for anything else. I show Frederick, who nods approvingly.

Frederick walks to the edge of the tent and then heads out. I follow him closely.

I count the tents as we walk by. There appear to be four big tents and six smaller ones. I just wish that some of the vehicles would have stuck around.

I look at Frederick. From the looks of him, he appears to be in his mid to upper fifties, a far cry from even Jake or Donna. I can see that, beneath his wooly beard, he seems to be a gentle person.

Frederick leads me to the highway, making me feel uncomfortable. He seems to do a good job gauging my reactions. "It's best to stay on the highway until we hear a vehicle coming. That way, we're less likely to get snake bit or lose our way."

I frown. "But isn't it more dangerous to stay on the roads? I mean, what's a snake bite or getting lost compared to losing your head?"

Frederick stops in his tracks. "Good point. I'm still not completely use to this New World Order deal. Perhaps we can stay in the woods around the road."

I nod. "That sounds better."

I hate to say it, but as nice as Frederick seems, he isn't the brightest. I would much rather take the risk of getting snake bit or getting lost than risk losing my head. Plus, I have a compass, so it's not like we'd really be lost. I decide to show it to him.

"That's good," he says, jovially. "We may need it."

And then it hits me. What I should be doing is looking for Jake and Donna. I mean, Jake cared enough about Donna to risk his life to try to find her, so why not try to do the same for them?

I look at Frederick. "You know, what I really want to do is to try to find my friends. You don't think the agents took them too far away do you?"

Frederick shrugs. "Hard to say. There's a detention center not far away from here, but I don't know if that is where they took them."

Hmm. I adjust the straps of the duffel bag in my hand. I can't help but feel sorry for Frederick. He is carrying two duffel bags to my one. Just in case we met anyone who needed assistance, he wanted to be ready. Anyway, I decided to check out the detention center. I run this by Frederick.

"I'll help you if that's what you really want to do," he says, earning a happy look from me. "I've been by there a few times before it was converted to a detention center for the unmarked."

"Really," I say.

Frederick nods. "Yep, and a good friend of mine use to work there years ago, before it became a detention center of course."

"That's great," I say, unable to contain my happiness. "Maybe we can do this yet."

"Probably not," Frederick says realistically, "but I guess it's worth a try."

I stare at the road ahead from the woods. "How far away is it?"

Frederick considers this. "About thirty minutes by vehicle, so you're looking at about an hour and a half or two-hour walk."

"That's not bad," I say, feeling a bubble of potential rising up inside of me. I look between Frederick and his duffel bags. "You wouldn't happen to have an agent's uniform in one of them would you?"

Frederick laughs. "I wish I did. I noticed that your friends were both wearing uniforms. But where they got them, I'd love to know. Still, don't guess it helped them too much, they still got caught."

"Yeah," I say, feeling my bubble deflating.

Frederick seems to notice this. "But that doesn't mean we should give up. Why I bet that between the two of us, we can give them agents a good run for their money."

I feel some better. I just feel like there are so many questions about breaking into a detention center. "For one," I say, getting Fredericks attention, "how do we go about getting inside? And when we do get inside, how do we know where to go?"

"We won't," Frederick says. "We'll just have to trust God that things will work out for us. It's funny that I said that. Before recently, I never believed in God. And then all hell started busting lose and what with the New World Order and the man getting shot and coming back to life, well, that convinced me."

"Yeah," I say. "I think it convinced a lot of people. The bad thing was, it was too late."

Frederick nods.

We keep walking as the sun continues to rise in the sky. I wipe sweat out of my eyes and swat at some gnats. I hate gnats. My mother always said that it'd be like paradise if it weren't for the mosquitoes and the gnats, and I think she was right.

I sigh. "How much longer?"

Frederick looks at the sun and then meets my eyes. "We should be getting there fairly quickly."

That sounds good.

After several more minutes of stepping over fallen trees and walking through brush, we finally spot the detention center just up ahead.

Frederick gives me a serious look. "We'll need to distract them somehow or be prepared to fight them. As for me, I'm no warrior. I just joined the Unmarked Battalion a couple weeks ago."

"So that's what you call yourselves," I say.

Frederick looks unhappy with himself. "Dang it, I wasn't supposed to give away our identity like that for security reasons."

I shrug. "I don't think it really matters now since your band has been dissolved."

"Yeah, I guess you're right," he says.

I set my duffle bag down on the ground and stretch my arms. I hunker down and take a bottle of water from my bag. I take a good long drink. If I am to have even the slightest chance of rescuing my friends, I'm going to need strength.

Frederick rummages around in one of his bags and takes out a bottle of water. He downs his in no time at all. I laugh inwardly as he reminds me of a big baby drinking from a bottle.

After eating a sandwich apiece, Frederick zips up his bag and sits them under a shade tree. I do the same with mine.

Frederick looks me straight in the eyes. "Let's do this."

I nod. And say a quick prayer too. Who knows, God might actually hear and act on our behalf.

CHAPTER 4 Kevin's Plan

Before we leave the woods behind, I begin to hatch a plan to recover Donna and Jake. Instead of just walking up to the building and probably getting caught, I decided to stage a scene. I run this by Frederick. He looks all but unconvinced.

"So let me get this straight," he says, looking doubtful. "First we try to lure out the agents by breaking a window. And then, once they're outside, we attack them. Attack them with what?"

"Our fists," I say, hearing the stupidity in my voice.

Frederick shakes his head. "It won't work. There are probably six or eight agents in there. No, the best thing to do would be to wait until one of them leaves and then head in."

I look at the lone car by the detention center. If one of us could get in the car, we could get inside, honk the horn a few times, wait until the agents come out, and then lure them away from the building. It might just work. I run this new plan by Frederick.

"Sounds better," he says. "Thing is, one of us needs to be somewhere around the building so that we can get through the door once the agents are lured away."

"Okay," I say. "I'll leave that to you."

I look Frederick in the eyes. "Are you ready?"

Frederick nods. "Yes. Let's do this."

Frederick and I leave the woods behind, feeling hopeful that our plan will work.

"Hey," I say, getting Frederick's attention. "Once we rescue Donna and Jake, let's all get in the car and hit the road."

"That's exactly what I was thinking," he says.

Good, at least we're both on the same page.

I head for the vehicle while Frederick heads for the building. As I walk, I'm aware of the grass crunching beneath my shoes. I just hope and pray that the door to the car isn't locked. Please don't let it be locked, I think.

I reach the driver's side of the car. I pull on the handle, and the door opens right up. Thank you, Jesus. I hurry up and get in. The key is in the ignition. Thank you, God. This might be easier than I thought.

I start the car and begin backing up. I lock the doors. I want the agents to follow me, but not be able to get inside the car.

I see Frederick hugging the corner of the building, waiting patiently on me.

I steer the car towards the front door, praying that this will work.

I give Frederick a quick thumbs up to tip him off, and then begin honking the horn. I press it several times.

I watch in fear as the door opens and an agent comes rushing out of the building.

I keep honking the horn. Eight, nine, ten times. Two more agents step out of the building and head right towards me.

I wait until there are no more agents coming out and then decide that it's time. I take my foot off the brake and begin steering away from the agents.

Slowly, I drive a little ways and then stop. I want the agents to try to get in, only without success.

In the rearview mirror, I see Frederick sneak into the building. Just like I thought, all the agents are around this car, trying to get in. The thing is, I'm not sure how Frederick, Donna, and Jake are going to be able to get in without getting caught by the agents. I need to come up with something else.

I wait patiently in the car while trying to think of a way to get rid of these agents and fast.

I look at the front door of the building. Come on Frederick, come on.

Finally, after several minutes, Frederick comes out of the building, followed behind a string of people. I look at the growing crowd, but no sign of Donna or Jake.

Seven people in all left the detention center. While many of them bolted off right away, heading towards the woods, I watch as Frederick heads to the woods behind the detention center. I suspect he'll follow me from within the woods until I get rid of these agents. So, without wasting any more time, I decided to slam my foot down on the gas pedal. I look behind me as I quickly leave the agents behind.

I look in the rearview mirror as the angry agents run back inside the building, probably to call for backup.

Just to make sure that none of the agents follow me, I drive a good quarter of a mile and then come to a stop. I scan the woods on the side of the road for any sign of Frederick and the others but see no sign of them. I imagine sirens splitting the air as the agent's barrel towards me.

I check the rearview mirror just in case agents are coming up behind me. I don't see anything. I look at the woods again and breathe a sigh of relief. Frederick and a couple others are quickly making their way towards me. I quickly unlock the doors. I roll down the passenger window.

Frederick gives me a worried look. "They weren't in there, but I freed every unmarked that was."

I nod. Great. I should have known that all this would be too easy.

I watch as two people open the back doors and climb inside. They are both unmarked.

I look at Frederick. "What about our duffel bags?"

"We'll just have to leave them. There's no going back now. It's too dangerous." he says.

I look at the gas gauge. I feel my spirits lifted. I turn to Frederick. "We have almost a full tank," I say.

"That's great," Frederick says. "We ought to be able to make it a long way then."

I look in the rearview mirror. I see the two guys in the back looking at me. "I'm Kevin, by the way. Glad we could help you."

"Yeah, thanks, man," says the dark haired guy. He looks like he is in his early twenties.

I look at the other guy. He has blond hair and a long nose.

"Yeah, thanks," he says.

I nod. "No problem. I'm just glad we could help. I just wish that my two friends would have been there with you."

"No you don't," says the dark haired guy. "Look," he says, showing me his right hand.

I feel my heart sink. He has taken the mark.

I look at the road ahead. I can't deny that I feel a little nervous. I never thought that we'd be rescuing anyone who already had the mark.

I look at the blond haired guy. "What about you," I say.

"I'm Panvil and I'm unmarked," he says.

"Panvil," I say.

He nods. "Yeah, that's my name. This guy beside me is Vince. And no, I haven't taken the mark like him."

I swallow hard. I still can't believe that I'm driving a car with a marked person inside of it. He could be dangerous.

The dark haired guy looks at me. "Stop the car. I want to show you something."

I look at Frederick. He nods approvingly. I stop the car.

The dark haired guy leans forward and shows me his hand. "Look," he says, wiping his fingers over the three black sixes."

I blink. It smeared the instant he touched it.

I can hardly believe my eyes. I look at him. "So you haven't taken the mark then."

Vince shakes his head. "Nope, just did this to try to fool the agents."

"But it didn't work," I say.

Vince shakes his head again. "Oh yes, it did. They were about to release me before you arrived."

"Really," I say, trying to stay in one lane.

Vince nods. "Yep."

I look at Panvil. "And what about you? What's your story?"

Panvil shrugs. "Nothing much just got rounded up when I least expected it. I was with two other people. They bolted the second your friend here broke us out of our cell."

I glance at Frederick. "Did you see any of the people you were with, you know, at the camp?"

Frederick shakes his head. "No, not one."

"Excuse me," Panvil says. "What were the names of the friends you were looking for?"

"Jake and Donna," I say.

Panvil swallows gives me a worried look. "I heard an agent mention them. Apparently, they were captured at some camp not far from here. I believe he said they were going to be shipped to Raftin Kriten."

"Where," I say, not really catching what he said.

"Raftin Kriten," he says again. "It's about a hundred and fifty miles from here. And no, I wouldn't go near that place for all the gold in the world. I hear there are over a hundred agents there."

I sigh. I look between the three of them, stopping on Frederick. "Then how do I go about rescuing my friends?"

Panvil gives me a sad look. "You don't. There's no way you could do what you just did. Breaking someone out of Raftin Kriten would be impossible unless you're prepared to take the mark of course."

I shake my head. "No, I don't want to do that."

I go around a hole in the road. It's strange, as happy as I should feel right now with having aided in setting seven people free, I feel worse now than I did. I just thought that Jake and Donna would be there, that's all.

"It wasn't in vain," Frederick says, slightly lifting my spirits. "We rescued six people that were likely going to be murdered. That's pretty good if you ask me."

I bang my head against the top of the seat. "I just wish we couldn't helped them."

Frederick nods. "Yeah, so do I. But look, maybe it's not God's will that either of them be rescued. Maybe it was God's will that they be captured and taken to Raftin Kriten."

"Maybe," I say, trying to keep it together. I can't deny that this whole experience is weighing heavily on me emotionally speaking.

Panvil leans forward, gives me a sideways glance. "I'm sorry about your friends, but I'm not going to say I'd rather it had been them here than us. Honestly, you're a God send."

I try to suppress a smile, but can't.

"You know," Frederick begins, "there might just be a way to rescue Donna and Jake yet."

"How" I say.

Frederick lets out a deep breath. "By doing what he tried to do, by dressing up as agents."

I steer the car around another pot hole.

I give Frederick what I'm sure is a nervous sideways look. "Alright, and if we decided to do this, where would we get an agents uniforms?"

"From agents of course," Frederick says.

I raise my eyebrows. "Like live ones?"

"Yep," Frederick says. "There's usually more of them alive than dead, though you may have tipped the scales a little in the right direction back there."

I want to laugh but decide not to. Honestly, those agents that I ran over are murderers. Even though I didn't want to hurt them, I really had no choice. It was either them or me. In this cruel and evil world, you have to stick up for yourself, because no one else will.

"You know," Frederick begins, "driving isn't the safest mode of travel. There are road blocks set up by agents to catch our kind, and if we get caught, God help us."

I glance at Frederick. "Then what would you suggest?"

"Walking," Frederick says. "We could hide in the brush and be much less likely to be discovered. The thing is, I have a bad leg and can't never walk more than a mile or so at a time before I have to take a long break."

I look in the rearview mirror at Panvil and Vince. I see them catch my eyes. "What do you two think? I mean, should we keep driving or get out and walk?"

Panvil looks thoughtful. "I think I'd keep driving. My brother and I came this way the other day and we didn't see an agent around anywhere."

"I agree," Vince says, looking dead serious. I wouldn't want to mess with him.

"Alright," I say. "Then we keep driving."

"Fine," Frederick says. "It's probably just as well. I think there are a lot of rattlesnakes around here anyway. It'd make walking dangerous."

So we keep on driving. I can't help but keep looking in the rearview mirror for any sign of mobilized agents.

As I drive, I think back to the time earlier when I ran over those agents. I can't help but feel a little bad about it. The thing is, those were murderers who would rather round us up for the mark or death than look at us.

I try not to drive too fast. The road is full of pot holes. I wish there were a church around so that I could talk to some of the other people who were left behind. I still can't believe it. I mean, I know that the Bible said that it was going to happen, but still. My mom use to say all the time that she was getting ready to leave here, and she did.

I can't believe that all the Christians are now in heaven, probably looking down on us, while we're here to face hell on earth. It just isn't fair. Or is it? I guess I had plenty of time to get ready, I just didn't do it.

I look at Frederick. His eyes are half open half closed. "Do you believe that all of that stuff in the Bible, in the book of Revelation is going to happen?"

Frederick turns towards me, looking very sleepy. He shrugs. "Difficult to say. I mean, it could take a long time to fulfill all of the end time prophecies of the Bible. I think there are some scriptures in Daniel that also talk about the end times, but I'm not for sure. Best thing to do is to try to get to Garbor and then worry about everything else later. If we can get there, then half of our problems will be over."

"Half," Panvil says behind me, causing me to jump. "I'd say that it's more like two-thirds. If we can get to Garbor, then we stand a good chance of riding out the many storms that are about to take place. From what I heard from a preacher friend not long ago was that there were going to be earthquakes, wars, and terrible things happen in the last days. And, while I'm not sure whether we're there now, we're very close."

Vince scoffs. "What do you mean 'very close'? How can you say that when you surely must know that we're there, at the end times I mean."

Panvil gives Vince a hard look. "Oh, so when did you become the Bible scholar? Last I heard, you spent more time with a bottle of whiskey than you did a Bible, so don't preach to me."

"Oh," Vince says. "Trying to cover up the fact that you were one of the town prostitutes are we."

Panvil grabs Vince's throat, looking murderous. "One more word out of you and you might not have to worry about getting your head chopped off."

"Enough," I say, jarring Frederick awake. "We all must have had problems because none of us made it in the Rapture, right? Now, if you two don't mind, I'd like for all of us to get along. In order to stand a better chance of making it to Garbor, we all need to have each other's back."

"Listen to the kid," Vince says to Panvil.

I want to tell him that I'm not a kid, but it wouldn't matter. What I do want, however, is for everyone to get along.

Panvil looks at me in the rearview mirror. I can see now how green his eyes are. He reminds me a lot of a friend I had years ago.

"I could do it," Panvil says.

I narrow my eyes at him in the rearview mirror. "Do what," I say.

"Rescue your friends," Panvil says. "Vince was right. I was a prostitute until fairly recently. And, while I'm not proud of what I did, I did make several acquaintances. I think I could easily trick some of the agents into giving me your friends for, well, favors."

You have got to be kidding. I look at Frederick. He looks just as alarmed.

I give Panvil a cautious look. "But wouldn't that be dangerous?"

Panvil nods. "Yeah, but I'm afraid it's the only way. Any other way and we'd likely all end up at Raftin Kriten."

I swallow hard. Panvil may be right. The last thing I want is to end up at Raftin Kriten. I remember reading stories of similar camps that use to exist years ago, and they were terrible places.

"So," I begin, looking at Panvil, "how would you go about doing this. I mean, how would you make yourself known without getting locked up yourself?"

"Easy," Panvil says with a sly smile. "But I would have to get locked up, at least for a short time. That way, I could be sure to work under cover. Agents are just like us, just as easily led astray if we're not careful. And, since I knew quite a few of them from my time at the detention center, I know what makes them tick."

"Alright," I say, looking between the road and Panvil. "Just don't get your head chopped off."

Panvil laughs. "Don't worry about me. I can get out of anything. What I want you to worry about is yourselves. It might take me several days to secure the release of your friends. Meanwhile, I expect you all to try to do everything you can to stay alive and well."

"Fair enough," I say, earning a glum look from Frederick. As for Vince, well, he looks somewhat pleased about Panvil's upcoming job. For a split second, I'd almost tell Vince to hit the road without us. But I don't feel like being that mean.

I keep on driving, careful to go around any debris in the road. So far, I've driven around dead trees, pot holes, and metal barrels. I just hope we can reach a safe place before too much longer. While I like driving, I don't like the idea of getting caught by an agent. Honestly, I'm surprised that we haven't met any other vehicles. I guess Panvil was right. There don't appear to be any agent's right around here.

Something important pops in my mind. I glance at Panvil. "How far away from Raftin Kriten do you want us to let you out? I mean, we don't want to get to close to that place."

"About a mile," Panvil says. "Since it is the next nearest stop on this road, about a mile should be fine."

I nod.

"What about food," Frederick says. "You should consider eating something before you take off. No telling how long you'll be before another good meal comes your way."

Panvil nods. "Sounds good."

After driving for several more minutes, we finally reach a new, glossy sign reading Raftin Kriten. I can't believe how quick the new order of things popped up after the Rapture. What looks like should have taken years was done in a matter of weeks.

I stop even with the sign. I tell Panvil to get out and grab some food from one of the duffle bags from the trunk.

Panvil gets back into the car a couple minutes later with a bottle of water and a sandwich. I wait nervously as he eats. I just want to get on with this whole recovery mission. The longer we wait, the more time that any amount of bad things could happen to my friends.

"Done," Panvil says after a couple of minutes. He looks at me in the rearview mirror. "Now, what you all should do is to leave this car behind and get off the road. Since we are this close to Raftin Kriten, you can expect agents to be patrolling the area.

I nod. "Where do you want to meet, once you get Donna and Jake, that is?"

Panvil looks at the large roadside sign. "How about here, by this sign. Or at least straight out in the woods from this sign. If you all could stay somewhere in the woods near this sign, then it'd make it easier to find you."

"Fine," I say, meeting Panvil's eyes. "We'll stay as close to this sign as we can without getting caught."

"Good luck," Frederick says. "And I say that with as much respect as I can muster."

Panvil nods. "Thanks. Meanwhile you three try to keep yourselves from getting caught. If you have to, take to the trees."

"That's a good idea," I say.

"Yeah," Frederick begins, "but let's hope that it doesn't come to that."

With one last reassuring look, Panvil opens the car door and starts walking straight ahead on the road. I bite down on my lower lip. I sure hope all goes well for him. I can see him getting himself out of trouble when it comes down to it, but as for rescuing two others, well, that's going to take some tact.

"We need to move," Vince says from the backseat. "The longer we stay here, the greater the chance of getting caught."

Good point. I get out and head to the back of the car. I take one of the duffel bags while Vince and Frederick take the other two.

With our bags in hand, we set off for the woods. I can't deny how anxious I am about this whole thing. I mean, what if things don't go as planned? There are just too many things that can go wrong. First off, Panvil is going to risk his life to do a good deed. Secondly, we're so close to Raftin Kriten that anything could go wrong. We could be caught in the blink of an eye if we're not careful.

As soon as we enter the woods, I start swatting mosquitoes. I wish there were some way to send them after agents only, as harsh a punishment as that would be. But the more I think about it, the more I wonder what all is going to happen in the coming weeks and months. We've already had one earthquake that split the ground in two. I just wonder when the giant locusts with stinging tails are going to be unleashed if they even do. I know I sound skeptical, but it is for a good reason. While I knew of many church going people back in the day, very few of them were ever healed or helped by going to church. From the looks of things, God didn't seem to care much about any of them.

Now that I think of it, there was one old lady who claimed that she was healed of blindness. But I don't know how reliable she is to use as a source. She could have easily made it all up.

"We need to find some big trees," Frederick says. "That'll give us more cover than these spindly little things. I wish that people hadn't been so greedy, that people hadn't cut down so many trees around here. It'll just make it harder to go unseen."

Nightfall comes faster than we'd like. I figure that Panvil has been arrested by now. I just hope the agents don't talk him in to taking the mark. I can see how appealing it could be with your life on the line.

"Let's camp here," Vince says, coming to a stop by a giant oak tree. "If we have to, we can sleep on the tree limbs. I noticed some rope in the trunk of the car that I can go and get if you'd like."

"Sounds good," I say. "Just be careful not to get caught."

Vince nods. "I'll be as careful as a fairy princess."

I laugh.

Vince turns around and sets off towards the car. I wonder how long it will take for the agents to find it. I just hope that Vince makes it to it before it is confiscated.

"You know," Frederick begins, "if Panvil is successful, if he does manage to secure your friend's release, then we're going to have a hard time feeding everyone. Not that I can't go without a meal or two, but we'll all have to eat eventually."

"Yeah," I say, sighing. "Let's just pray that everything goes well. While I'm not yet convinced that prayer works, I hope it does."

Frederick nods. "Yeah, I know what you mean."

Frederick and I decide to skip our evening meal so that we can make our food last longer.

I see movement in a nearby tree. I look closely and see a gray squirrel sitting on a limb watching us closely. I wish I had that pistol of Jakes. Sooner or later we're going to need more food.

I turn to Frederick. He gives me a knowing look. I just wish there was some way to get that squirrel. It'd make enough food for all three of us, granted that we eat small amounts.

Another thing I wish I had was that map of Jakes. It's hard to tell where we're at, at what district we're at without it. That makes it harder to tell if we're getting close to Garbor or not. From what I heard, Garbor was nestled somewhere in the Rocky Mountains. And right now, I think we are somewhere in district four, which would put us several hundred miles or so away from Garbor.

I sigh. Everything is so complicated. I don't know, part of me thinks it'd be a heck of a lot easier just to take the mark and be done with it. But then again, if what the Bible says is true, I'd lose my soul. And since the earthquake, I'm leaning a little more towards believing the Bible is the truth.

"Got it," Vince says, appearing with a hand full of rope. "Fortunately there weren't any agents around the car. I suspect that they'll find it soon enough."

Vince hands me the rope. I take it as a thought forms in my mind. I wonder if there are bears around here. It'd probably be wise to hoist our food up into the tree with us. I'd sure hate to lose what little food we've got. But then again, since pretty much everything is canned, I doubt a bear can smell it. I guess it'll be alright to leave everything on the ground by the tree.

I look between Frederick and the rope. "How much do you think we'll need," I say.

"At least three or four feet," Frederick says.

"Here," Vince says, handing me a knife. "You can cut it with this."

I take the knife and measure out what looks like four feet. I'm probably off a few inches, but all well.

Now that I have enough rope cut for each of us to tie ourselves to a limb, I lay the remaining rope down at the foot of the tree. After handing rope to Frederick and Vince, I look around to make sure nothing is lying around carelessly. Everything appears to be in order.

I look at Frederick and Vince. "You guys can go first. I'll take one of the bottom limbs."

Vince begins scaling the tree like a pro. I'm glad because I didn't want to argue about who gets what limb as I'm too tired.

I wait a little while for Frederick to get situated before climbing. It looks like my limb is about six feet off the ground. That's not too bad. I was just a little leery about taking a limb high up in the tree. I don't trust my knots enough.

I situate myself on the limb and then wrap the rope around my legs. I lean back against the tree as I tie a knot. I test the knot by pulling on the ends of the rope. It is secure. I breathe a sigh of relief.

I try looking through the limbs above me to where Vince and Frederick are. "Is everyone alright up there?"

Both of them answer favorably. I just hope that nobody falls out of the tree and breaks their neck. That'd be the worst thing that could happen.

I look up at the sky between an opening in some tree limbs. Several stars twinkle through the opening. I yawn. I hope we have a good day tomorrow. It'd be great to get Jake and Donna back in our company. The bad thing is, Jake won't have his pistol the next time I see him. I imagine it was one of the first things that were confiscated from him. I bet he's glad he gave me the watch and compass. Without a doubt, the agents would have confiscated both items.

I feel sleep pulling me under. I closed my eyes briefly and will myself to dream pleasant dreams. In situations like this, the conditions are ripe for nightmares. I wish I had a glass of water.

I see a giant waterfall off in the distance. Frederick advises me against going there as it could be a focal point for agents. I decide to press my luck.

I sniff the air. I can smell the sweet smell of the water. It fills my nostrils like a fragrant bloom. I jump over a tree on the ground.

I swallow hard. My throat is dry, and my stomach is growling. Maybe there's some fish at the foot of the waterfall. That'd be great.

The closer I get to the waterfall the more thirsty I become. I hope there aren't any agents around. I hum a tune as I quicken my pace.

I arrive at the stream flowing away from the waterfall and drop to my knees. I cup my hands together and get a drink of water.

I spit it out. It is blood. I rise to my feet. The waterfall is a giant flow of blood. I wonder how many people were killed to get this much blood.

I hear a voice somewhere behind me. I turn around and listen as it gets closer.

"Is there anyone there," says a voice. "There's four agents and a pack of hounds coming this way. If anyone's there, you had better get moving."

"Get down," says another voice. "Vince, Kevin, we gotta go."

I hear dogs barking off in the distance. It sounds like they're heading this way.

Someone shakes me. "Wake up. Quick. They're after us."

I open my eyes. I turn around and see Vince heading down the tree beside me.

"Hurry, no time to explain," he says.

The barking gets closer and closer. I untie the knot above my knees and let the rope fall to the ground.

"Hurry up Kevin," Frederick says.

I grab hold of the limb and work my way to the tree trunk. I hurry down the tree as loud curses fill the night air around us. I flinch.

As soon as I make it to the ground, I see Frederick and Vince take off running. A split second later they're gone, and I can't see them.

"Where are you," I say above the approaching noise of the dogs.

"Over here," Frederick says loudly.

I make my way to his voice.

A hand comes out of the darkness and grabs me.

"We gotta run," Frederick says.

I nod as if he can see me.

I set off running after Frederick and Vince. All I can see are two black objects swiftly moving through the darkness.

I turn around and hear the dogs getting closer. And then it hits me. They're after us.

I press forward with all of my might. I dodge trees right to left and try not to trip. This is bad. If the agents catch up with us, it will be all over.

I run through a stream of water and come to a quick decision. In order to avoid getting caught, I need to throw off the dogs. I need to cover my tracks.

"This way," I yell, hoping that the others can hear me.

I set off down the stream, hoping and praying that the dogs go a different direction. I run over several jagged rocks, nearly tripping.

I thrust one of my feet into a pool of water. Then the other foot. I stop, trying to see how big the hole of water is. I don't want to drown, but I don't want to get caught either. I blink a few times and then see the black pool of water before me come into better view.

I decide to take the risk and go through the water, hoping that it'll throw the dogs off. I need to cover up my scent.

Within a blink of an eye, I feel myself sinking in the water. I'm going to have to swim. Dang it. I was hoping it wouldn't be this deep.

Without giving it another thought, I start to swim. This should help cover my trail. I just hope that Frederick and Vince followed me.

I swim to the other side of the pool of water and rise to my feet. I listen for the dogs.

They're still coming.

I take off running down the creek bed, sharp pains jabbing the soles of my shoes. I don't know how much more of this I can take.

"I'm right behind you," comes a voice.

It is Frederick.

Without looking back, I keep pressing forward, determined to throw off the dogs.

I run with all my might. I think of the choice that would arise from getting caught. Either I would take the mark of the beast, or I would lose my head.

I blink and then see another pool of water coming up. Again, I don't know how deep it is. I'm nearly out of breath.

I hit the water running. I feel the slippery rocks beneath my shoes beckoning me forward.

I see a tree root rising up from the water, next to the bank. I decided to make my way to it. Already I can tell that this pool of water isn't as deep as the other one was. The water isn't even at my shoulders yet, and I'm half way through.

I grab hold of the tree root and hunker down. I turn around and come face to face with Frederick.

I listen closely for any sign of the dogs. Nothing. Maybe we've thrown them off.

And then I hear them. Several dogs bark like they've found something.

Oh no, Vince.

I look at Frederick in the eyes. "We have to go back," I say, letting go of the tree root.

"No," Frederick says, grabbing hold of my arm. "You'll be caught. Thank God that we haven't been caught yet."

I take a deep breath. Frederick is right. We can't go back. If we do, we'll surely be caught. It's bad enough that Vince appears to have been caught.

I hear someone screaming. It is Vince. It sounds like the dogs are working him over. Oh God, please let it stop, please.

And then it does.

Everything goes silent.

"They've got him," I say.

Frederick throws up an index finger at his lips for me to be quiet. He nods behind me.

I turn around and see someone moving this direction.

"I think they went this way," says a voice.

It is an agent.

I lower myself into the water and hug the tree root. Frederick does the same thing.

I see someone standing at the pool of water, shining a flashlight down this way. I decided to dunk my head under the water.

Water floods my ears, but I see no other option right now. I try to hold my breath as long as I can.

In my mind's eye, I picture an agent wading through the water, heading in this direction. A rock...I need a rock. I can use it to defend myself if I have to. I bend down and grab hold of the first sizable rock my hand comes across.

I don't think I can take it much longer. I let out a little air, hoping that I don't have to use this rock.

I hear someone mumble something above the water.

Next second, a hand grabs hold of my arm and jerks me from the water.

I come up out of the water gasping for breath.

"They're gone," Frederick says. He looks shaken. "Good thinking by the way. I did the same thing."

I breathe a sigh of relief. I wipe the slime off my face. Clearly, this water hole is stagnant. It smells bad too.

"What should we do," I say.

"Stay here a while longer," Frederick says.

I nod. I don't see or hear any sign of the dogs or agents that were on our paths a few moments ago.

I look at the holes in and around the tree roots. I hope there aren't any snakes or spiders. I move away just in case.

But Frederick pulls me back into the bank. "Stay here for the cover. We blend in with the roots right now."

I nod. I move back into the tree roots where God knows what is slithering around.

I look up at the sky. I can spot a few openings among the trees, allowing small windows into the heavens.

After a few minutes, Frederick points upstream and says, "that way."

I hug the bank, grabbing hold of the tree roots for cover and balance. I imagine a snake sinking its fangs into my hand. I press my eyes shut for a second, then open them.

We leave the water hole behind, making me feel better. We had better keep heading in this direction. It wouldn't surprise me one bit if an agent weren't lurking somewhere downstream from us, just waiting to make another capture.

I see a deep ravine on the bank just up ahead. I point to it, getting Fredericks attention.

"There," I say, making my way towards the ravine.

As soon as I get to the ravine, I sprawl out and feel the water slowly draining from my shoes. I feel disgusting.

Frederick lays down beside me, looking like I feel.

Minutes roll by, leaving Frederick and me at the mercy of the forest around us. I feel sleep pulling me under. I feel several rocks poking me in the back, telling me to move on, but I'm too sleepy to listen to them.

What feels like hours later, I wake to Frederick sitting up, whittling a cane pole.

"Where'd you get that," I say, sitting up.

"Just upstream from here," he says. "Got you one too."

"Thanks," I say, stifling a yawn.

Frederick looks beat. "We need to get moving soon. I suspect that that agent will be back here at some point to see if we're still around."

"Yeah," I say, not wanting to get up.

"Here," Frederick says, handing me his knife. "You need to do the same to yours. We need weapons, just in case."

I nod. I pick up the cane pole, which is about as large as one of my index fingers and start whittling on the end of it. This is a good idea.

And then it begins to sink in. I stop and look up at Frederick. "Our supplies, everything is gone."

Frederick nods. "We can't go back. It'd be too dangerous. I bet there's agents swarming the area where we left our stuff."

It makes me angry to think about agents getting our stuff. I'd rather it all be blown to bits than see any of our stuff fall into the hands of the likes of them.

After several minutes of whittling, I run a finger along the sharp edge, pleased with my work.

"Let's go," Frederick says, getting up.

I follow suit.

"So what do we do now," I say.

Frederick looks tired and serious. "If we want to live, we need to get as far away from here as possible."

"But what about Panvil," I say. "What if he manages to come back and we're not there?"

Frederick shrugs. "Can't help that. We have to look out for ourselves first and foremost."

I can see what he means, but still. I swallow hard. "What if we were to go to Raftin Kriten ourselves."

Frederick frowns. "What do you mean?"

I take a deep breath. "I mean, why don't we go to him instead of him coming to us. We could monitor the area for him and then meet up with him when he comes out."

Frederick shakes his head. "Too dangerous. There'd be too many agents around the vicinity. We'd get caught. And besides, we don't even know where we are from here."

I bite down on my lower lip. And then I remember. I have a compass. Jake gave it to me just before he left that night. I reach into my pocket, hoping that it's still there.

I feel my fingers grasp it. I pull it out and show it to Frederick.

His eyes light up. "Where'd you get that?"

I tell him.

"That's great," he says. "As long as we keep heading west, we'll be bound to make it to Garbor eventually. I suspect we will run across a lot of places where we can load up on supplies between here and there."

Yeah. "I just hope we can find another vehicle. The Rocky Mountains are still a long ways off."

Frederick nods.

We leave the stream behind and stand on the bank overlooking it. I didn't realize it was that deep last night when we were running through it.

"So where to from here," Frederick says.

I look at the compass. "That way," I say, pointing. "That way is west."

"Or," Frederick begins, "we could just walk this creek all the way to the highway. Then, we can cross the highway and head into the forest on the other side. That way, we'd be a safer distance from the tree where we left our supplies."

I nod. "Good idea."

So, we set off down the stream, on the opposite bank, that we ran through last night.

Cane poles in hand; we walk as fast as the forest allows us. There are huge rocks and fallen trees every so many feet. Honestly, it looks like a wind storm came through here not long ago. Some of the fallen trees still have green leaves on them.

After what feels like hours of walking, Frederick and I finally make it to the highway. There is no sign of the car anywhere. But since we appear to have exited the forest in a different location, that doesn't surprise me.

I look at the highway with both a longing and apprehension. As much as I'd like to be able to stay on it, it is unsafe. It is far easier to walk on the highway than it is to wander through a forest.

We quickly crossed the highway and head into the forest on the other side. At least we now have weapons, though not very good ones. I just hope we don't have to use them. I'm not sure how sturdy this cane pole would be if I had to drive it into human flesh.

Now in the forest, I have to ask Frederick, "should we stay here or keep moving?"

"Keep moving," Frederick says. "We need to try to get as close to Raftin Kriten as we can without getting caught."

"But what about our supplies," I say. "I mean, I could use a drink of water right now, and we have absolutely no water or food for that matter."

Frederick looks sympathetic. "We'll find some, just you wait."

I nod. I hope we do and soon. I'm not sure how much longer I can make it without water. While I'm not hungry right now, I am very thirsty.

As we move along in the edge of the forest, I can't help but wonder if we're doing the right thing. I mean, what if Panvil never shows up? What if we never see Panvil or Jake again for that matter. Not to mention Donna. I decide to run this by Frederick.

Frederick shakes his head from side to side. "There are pros and cons, you're right there. But if you want to get your friends back, this is our best chance. Otherwise, we can head west and make for Garbor."

I swallow hard. As much as I want to get Jake and Donna back, I don't want to wind up in a bad way myself. So far since I left home, I've met many people, several of which have gotten caught by agents. Leslie was the first, followed by Jake and Donna. I just don't know what to do. I don't want to risk losing Frederick, or getting caught myself, but if I want to get my friends back, I have no choice. I have to do something.

Frederick stops, gives me a measured look. "So what will it be? Should we press forward towards Raftin Kriten, or do you want to head straight for Garbor?"

That is a tough question. The thing is, I don't want to get my head chopped off over trying to get my friends back. It's too risky.

I bite down on my lower lip. "I don't know. I just don't know what to do. Part of me wants to see if Panvil is successful, and part of me wants to stay as far away from Raftin Kriten as possible."

Frederick nervously pulls at his beard. "I guess we could wait right here for Panvil. I'm just now sure if he could find us this far out."

"Good point," I say. "We need to try to get closer to Raftin Kriten. Do you know the way?"

Frederick nods. "Yes, but I don't know how close I want to get to it. I'd say we're about five miles from Raftin."

I swallow. "That far. How far do you think we were when we stopped the car yesterday?"

"About two miles out," Frederick says. "Look, if you really want to try to find Panvil, then I'll help you."

I try to suppress a smile. "Fine, let's see how close we can get without getting caught."

Frederick nods. "Okay. But if we do get caught, don't give up, there could always be help on the horizon."

I nod and wave a hand in front of me. "Lead the way."

CHAPTER 5 Raftin Kriten

Frederick gives me a polite nod and then takes off. I fall into step behind him.

I sure hope that Panvil is successful. I'd feel much better having Jake and Donna back. I felt more secure with them at my side.

"So," Frederick begins, "what catastrophe do you think will smite us next. Will it be hailstones or giant locusts?"

I laugh, though I know I should take all this more seriously. The thing is, I am not yet convinced. Maybe there is more to the sudden disappearance of all the Christians. "To be honest, I've been doing some thinking about the giant locusts, and I don't think I want to see them at all."

Frederick grins. "Oh come on surely you're up to getting stung and then making grasshopper chocolates out of them. Can you imagine how much chocolate it'd take to cover a giant grasshopper?"

"No," I say. "And I hope I never find out. Let's hope we can make it to Garbor before anything else unusual happens."

"You and me," Frederick says with a cautious gleam in his eyes. "I can tell that you aren't yet sold on the matter of everything that's been happening, but you will be. I was just like you a few weeks ago until I witnessed over a hundred people lose their heads not far from here."

I feel my jaw drop. "You mean you actually witnessed beheadings?"

Frederick nods. "Yes, and I can tell you that it was no fun. I just happened to be in the wrong place at the wrong time. I was just driving through with a buddy of mine, and we saw all these people in a line, so we decided to stop and see what was going on. From a hidden location, we witnessed person after person lose his head. Even little children."

I feel taken aback. "Even little children," I say, hardly believing my ears.

"Yes, and it was awful. First thing they were asked was whether or not they would pledge allegiance to Vladimir. Then, they were given one last chance to take the mark on their right hand or forehead. Very few of them took the mark. So, most of them were put to death."

I swallow hard. Maybe we shouldn't try to see how close we can get to Raftin Kriten. I'd like to keep my head for as long as I can.

I give Frederick what I'm sure is a very serious look. "Do you think we're doing the right thing, you know, trying to reunite with Panvil and the others?"

"Can't say," Frederick says. "I just know that if you want to see your friends again, this is the best possible way to see it done."

I stare at my cane pole weapon. "I just wish we were armed with better weapons. I wish Jake had given me his pistol before he set out the other night."

"Anyone would in times like these," Frederick says. "You're a good kid, Kevin. I wish I were as level headed when I was your age."

I frown. "I missed the Rapture."

Frederick shrugs. "Lots of people did, but that doesn't make them bad people. That just means that they probably didn't accept Jesus Christ as their Lord and Savior."

I stare miserably at the ground. "I wish I had if nothing more than to be in heaven right now instead of down here. I wonder what it felt like flying away into the heavens?"

"Hard to say," Frederick says. "But I will say this: The true Christians are all gone, and here we are stuck in one of the darkest points of history. If I had any idea how bad all this was going to be, I would have said yes to Jesus years ago. But then again," Frederick says, "the thing that really bothers me is how is it possible to defy gravity and wind up in heaven?"

I shake my head. "I don't know. I guess God had a way to do it. Otherwise everyone would still be here on earth."

"Yeah," Frederick says. "Guess so."

Frederick and I continue walking on for the longest time. I begin to wonder if I'll ever get a drink of water.

And then it happens. In a split second, we find ourselves hanging upside down from a large tree limb. I feel everything fall out of my pockets and hit the ground.

Oh no, now we're in big trouble.

"Who is this we have here," says a curious voice.

I try to find its source, but can't. It sounds like it might have come from above us in the tree.

"Let's see," says the curious voice. "It looks like I have two males in my custody."

I swallow hard. This is not good. Dang it. Why didn't we see the snare?

I blink and then come face to face with a woman.

"Who are you," I say, staring into her blue eyes. She's really quite attractive, even if I am upside down.

"That's none of your business," she snaps. "The question is, who are you?"

I give her a hard look. "That's none of your business."

She laughs. "Stubborn aren't you handsome. Well, if that's the way you want it perhaps I'll just leave you two hanging here for the agents."

I feel frantic. "No, please. My name is Kevin and this here is Frederick."

She gives me a small smile. "And what brings you to this area? Why come this close to danger?"

"You mean Raftin Kriten," I say.

She nods. "Exactly."

"We're looking for someone," I say.

"Just someone," she answers back.

I shake my head. "Several people actually. A friend of ours is supposed to meet us in these woods."

"Really," she says. "That's interesting. Who might I ask are these friends of yours, perhaps I know them?"

"Panvil," I say, feeling dizzy. I've never spent this long upside down in my life. "And at least two others."

She gives me a steady gaze. "Never heard of him. But I really don't care."

"Then why ask," I say.

"It's my business to know things," she says. "I buy and sell information for a living you see. That's what keeps me alive."

I try to take a deep breath but am having problems.

"Fine," I say, wanting down. "Let us down, and I'll give you an ear full."

I hear the long blade slice through the air, cutting us down. I fall to the ground with a thud. I massage my shoulder.

"Let's hear it," says the woman, who I now see has shoulder length blond hair and a small scar on her face.

I nod. "I'm looking for my friends like I said. One of their names we already told you. As for the others, give us your name first, and I'll give you theirs."

"Mary," she says. "Now tell me, how did you two find yourselves out in the middle of nowhere with no supplies?"

"They were taken," I say. "Or at least we think they were. We had to set out running from the dogs they put on us."

"You mean the agents," Mary says.

I nod. "Yeah. There were three of us until last night. One of our company, Vince, was taken captive. Or at least we think so."

Mary nods. "I'm sorry to hear that. I'm more sorry for your friends. If they're in Raftin Kriten, then they're probably already dead."

I close my eyes for a second. When I open them, Mary hands me a silver bottle and tells me to drink. So I do.

I drink and drink and then think of Frederick, so I stop. I look at Mary. "Do you care if he has a drink too?"

"Go ahead," she says. I give the bottle to Frederick. "There's much more where that came from."

I frown. "Where did you get it?"

"From a spring not far from here," Mary says. "The waters so cold it gives you a headache if you drink it right from the spring. Do you want me to take you to it?"

I shrug. "We don't have anything to store water in."

"That's fine," Mary says. "It just so happens that I have two other bottles."

"You do," I say, feeling stupid.

Mary nods. "Yes, and for the right information, I'll give them to you."

I sigh. "I already told you why we're here and what we have planned. What more can we tell you?"

"There's always more," says Mary almost sarcastically. "Follow me if you want to go to that spring I told you about. If not, we'll part ways here."

"Take us to the spring," I say politely.

Mary nods. "Like I said, it's not far."

Frederick, like me, looks as if he could use another drink. I just wonder what we're going to have to tell Mary in order to secure us those two bottles.

I fall into step beside Mary. "So, what brings you to these parts?"

"Adventure," Mary says. "I'm on my way to Garbor. Let me guess, that's where you all are heading as well."

I nod. "Which is why I want my friends back. I want to go there with them. There's safety in numbers."

"But also danger," Mary says. "Sometimes too many people attracts too much attention."

"I haven't thought of it like that," I say.

Mary looks at me like I'm stupid. "Well, you should. After I lead you two to the spring I told you about, you're on your own. But before I give you the bottles, you're going to have to tell me more."

"Okay," I say, not caring about holding anything back.

"For example," Mary begins, "you could tell me your whole name and where you came from."

I swallow. In these times, I like to keep that information to myself. But I can see that, in order to secure for ourselves the bottles, I'm going to have to do some talking.

"My name is Kevin Trill. I'm from district three and left home to escape capture."

Mary looks pleased. "Sounds like me. I too left home that I might find refuge elsewhere. What about your family? Are you the only one left?"

I nod. "My mom and dad went missing about the time that everyone else did. Honestly, I don't know if it was the Rapture, or something else."

"Oh it was the Rapture," Mary says. "I can personally testify to that. One second I was talking to my little girl, and the next second she disappeared right in front of my eyes."

I swallow. "Really? I mean, I thought there were other possibilities, like kidnapping and stuff."

Mary laughs. "Kidnapping? Do you really think that millions of people were all kidnapped?"

I turn to the ground, feeling stupid. "I guess not. I just didn't know what to think."

Mary gestures to Frederick. "What about him?"

Frederick clears his throat. "I'm Frederick Longsworth from district three."

Mary looks more curious. "So Frederick, what brings you to a place like this?"

"Survival," Frederick says. "The group of men and women that I was working with until recently participated in rescue missions. That's how I met Kevin and his friends, they wandered into our camp."

Mary nods. "Interesting. If you don't mind me asking," she says, stopping to look at Frederick, "how is it that you ended up with Kevin here?"

Frederick looks like he's growing tired of questions, and I don't blame him. "I hid when a group of agents stormed our camp. I found Kevin hiding in the edge of the woods by our camp. His friends had been captured by the agents."

Mary gives me a sad look. "So, that's your story. You're on the run, like me."

I nod. "Yeah, and once we meet back up with my friends, we're going straight to Garbor."

Mary raises her eyebrows. "No one ever goes straight to Garbor. You have to go through countless miles of territory even more inhospitable than this. From what I've been told, it is a fool's journey. If you ever make it there, you'll be able to count yourself among the lucky few."

I let out a deep breath that I didn't realize I was holding.

Mary can tell that she popped my bubble. "I'm sorry dear. I truly am. But it's good that you know the truth. Better to learn it now than have to wonder why things seem so set against you later."

I guess so. Without another word, Mary turns around and heads towards the spring. I almost wish that we hadn't met up with her. But then again, we were in need of a drink of water.

We arrive at the spring a couple minutes later. Mary takes off her backpack and unzips it. Next second, she pulls out two stainless steel bottles and hands them to us. I give her a grateful nod.

I walk over to the spring and kneel down. I lower my bottle into the water and watch as it flows into the opening. Admittedly, I do feel better now that we have this good water. I was afraid that we'd have to backtrack and drink out of that muddy creek.

I rise to my feet a moment later and put the cap back on the bottle. I watch as Frederick takes a big drink from his bottle and then refills it. At least it's cool around this spring. If I weren't so concerned about meeting Panvil, I'd probably stay here a while. There's probably wild game that we could catch and eat around here.

With our water bottles filled, Frederick and I turn to Mary, who looks impatient. I guess she wants to get as far away from us as possible. From the way she sounded earlier, she doesn't feel comfortable traveling with anybody other than herself for fear of getting caught.

"Well," Mary begins, "if you don't mind, I think I'll part ways with you all here. I'm anxious to get to Garbor as soon as possible, or at least before the next disaster strikes."

"The next disaster," I said questioningly.

Mary nods. "Like that earthquake the other day. That was nothing compared to what's about to come on the earth. No, I suspect that, before it's all said and done, we'll wish we were dead."

I swallow hard. I hope she's wrong. She seems so confident when she speaks.

Mary extends a hand to me. "Well, if we ever make it to Garbor, then hopefully I'll see you there."

I shake her hand. She then shakes Frederick's hand.

After filling her own water bottles, Mary heads out the way we came. I suspect that she knows the area better than she let on.

I turn back to Frederick. "So it's just me and you again. Do you think she was right, Mary?"

"About what," Frederick says.

"About all the disasters," I say, trying not to talk too loud. Mary is still within range of hearing us if I spoke too loudly. I lean into Frederick. "Really, she seemed like the gloomy type. Doom and gloom seem like her best friends right now."

Frederick laughs. "Yeah, I got the same impression. Nevertheless, I think she's right. Before this is all said and done, I think we'll be lucky to get away with our lives."

"We could always take the mark," I say jokingly.

"And wind up in hell," Frederick says, also jokingly. I guess we shouldn't be joking about such things, but after talking to Mary, who was so serious, it feels good to joke some.

Frederick and I set off the way we came. At least this spring wasn't far away from the highway. If it had been, we might have needed Mary to lead us back out the way we came.

I look at Frederick. "What do you think is going to happen next? I mean, what kind of disaster do you think is going to strike next?"

Frederick shrugs. "Hard to say, but I believe that something like darkness and locusts is on the horizon, granted that we are in the last days."

After listening to Mary, I do feel more compelled to believe that the Rapture has actually happened. It's strange until I met her, I was still wishy washy about it all. But now I think there's something to it. Where there's smoke, there's usually fire."

As we approach the highway, I can hear a vehicle heading this way. I hunker down and watch as Frederick copies me.

As the car drives by slowly, I look at the driver and nearly pass out.

"It's Panvil," I say, rising to my feet. "He's looking for us. Come on."

I leave the woods behind shouting for Panvil to stop. And he does. Fortunately, he wasn't going very fast.

I run up to the car, feeling crazy and lightheaded. Who would have thought that it would have been this easy?

"Hey," I say, looking at the passenger side. No one is there. "Where's Jake?"

Panvil smiles. "Lucky for you there was only one Jake at the compound."

Panvil quickly gets out of the car and heads to the back. He presses a button and then stands to the side. I step up to the trunk of the car and see Jake laying down and smiling. I'm just glad that the trunk was big enough to accommodate him.

Jake gets out, looking pleased to see me. "I had a feeling you would try to do something to rescue me. When one of the agents told me that a certain Panvil had secured my release, I nearly passed out. He didn't tell me about you until we got to the car."

I give Jake a big hug. "Good to see ya," I say. "Hey, where's Donna?"

Jake gives me a sad frown. "I never saw her. They must have taken her to a different compound. The only person I knew at Raftin Kriten was Leslie. She took the mark and was let go before I was released."

I swallow hard. "She did what? How could she? Didn't she know that you could lose your soul over it?"

Jake shrugs. "Didn't seem to faze her. I was standing in line when I saw an agent tattoo her right hand. The same agent asked me if I wanted one, so I said I'd have to think about it. Everyone else who said straightforwardly that they wouldn't take the mark was put to death."

"Just like that," Frederick says with a question in his tone of voice.

Jake nods. "Yep. What was really bad was that I had to watch every person who didn't take the mark be put to death. I counted over three hundred people who lost their heads."

I feel light headed myself. I can't believe that Jake was so close to death. I'm just glad to have him back. But about Donna...

"Do you think that Donna was already put to death," I say. "Like before you had to watch, I mean?"

Jake shakes his head. "No. I asked Panvil to check the registry and Donna wasn't on it."

"Then where could she be," I say, feeling bad for Donna.

Jake looks around us, paranoid. "It's hard to say, but I don't think we should just stand here and talk anymore. The agent that let us go said that if another agent caught us, then we'd be out of his hands."

"His," I say, frowning. I thought Panvil just secured deals with female partners. I never thought about him being friendly with a man.

Looking as if he knows what I'm thinking, Panvil says, "it's what it took to get your friend out of that place. Honestly, I have no desire for men."

I hope he's telling the truth. But then again, God can save anyone.

Panvil pats me on the shoulder as he walks back around to the driver's side of the car. Jake, looking pleased to see me gets out of the trunk and heads for the passenger's side. I get into the back of the car with Frederick.

As soon as Panvil turned around and saw everyone in the car, he headed out. But hey, I forgot to tell him about Vince. And Panvil didn't ask about him.

I take a deep breath. "Panvil," I say, getting his attention. He has gray eyes that look sort of sad. "I forgot to tell you about Vince. He…"

"I already know," Panvil interrupts. "He…also took the mark."

Dang it. What is wrong with these people?

Looking as if he can read my mind, Panvil says, "I saw him take the mark just before I secured Jake's release. Honestly, I wasn't surprised. Vince never came across as the religious type."

I frown. "But surely he knew. I mean, about losing your soul."

Panvil shakes his head from side to side. "Maybe he did, maybe he didn't. Oh, and how was it that you all ended up so far away from where I last saw you?"

I look at Frederick, quietly passing the question to him.

"We didn't at first," he says. "It wasn't until the agents set dogs on us that we found ourselves running for our lives. We didn't know where we were going, just that we were trying to throw off the dogs from tracking us. Not long after that, we met a woman named Mary. She gave us these here drinking bottles and led us to a spring just for answering her questions."

Panvil frowns. "Really?"

Frederick nods. "She seemed friendly as if she knew us or something."

Jake turns around and looks between Frederick and I. "Was she pretty?"

Now Frederick looks at me, silently passing the questions. I shrug. "I guess you could say that. She wasn't ugly."

Jake grins, showing his nice teeth. "Did you uh…get a chance to kiss her?"

I frown. "No, and why would you ask something like that?"

Jake shrugs. "Just curious. I'm just surprised that she wasn't attracted to you, you being such a good looking guy and all."

"Jake," I say, slightly chidingly. I want to tell him that he looks better than I do, but I decide not to. I don't want him to get the wrong impression about me.

"So what was it like," I say, changing the story.

Jake considers this. "Oh, you mean Raftin Kriten? Well, it wasn't no picnic if that's what you're wondering. All I had to eat was stale bread and watered down soup. One man died not long after I arrived, so I was able to convince the agents to give me his meal portion along with my own."

Panvil looks at Jake out of the corner of his eye. "Really," he says. "I...guess it was because you are so handsome. I can't imagine why a guy...or was it a woman?"

Jake nods. "It was. And boy was she lovely. I nearly had her convinced at one time to let me out, but she told me that that would cost her her job and possibly her life."

Panvil looks between Frederick and I. "What about you two? How did you manage to throw the dogs off your trail?"

Again, not wanting to talk right now, I toss the question over to Frederick. He looks more than pleased to answer it.

"There was a creek," Frederick says. "We must have run a mile down that creek bed until we finally got to where we couldn't run anymore. So, having found a deep hole of water, we decided to use it to our advantage. We grabbed hold of some tree roots while we hoped and prayed that the dogs would lose our scent. And they must have because they never came into that hole of water after us."

"Good," Panvil says. "I was worried about you all."

Frederick catches Panvil's eyes in the rearview mirror. "We were worried about you too. Worried sick, honestly. I kept seeing you lose your head in my mind's eye."

Panvil laughs. "That must have looked funny."

Frederick laughs. "Yeah, it did."

I shake my head with a laugh. I lean forward to talk to Jake. "So, tell us more about what it was like at Raftin. Besides the food, what were the other accommodations?"

Jake turns around to face me. "Bad. I had to use the restroom in front of everybody. That's the way everyone had to do. And I couldn't sleep at night for all the rats running over my body."

I swallow. "Rats? That sounds terrible."

Jake nods. "It was. I thought about eating them, but the smell of feces was so strong that it turned me off. Plus, the rats ate dead flesh."

"Really," I say, not really wanting to hear more.

"Yeah," Jake says. "That would have been the hardest thing to get past in order to eat one of them. But I told myself that if I had to stay in there much longer, I might consider it."

Jake looks me over, like a big brother. "So, you look to be in good shape considering everything you've been through. Don't still have that compass I gave you do you."

I shake my head. "No, it fell out of my pocket when we were suddenly yanked upside down."

Jake narrows his eyes at me. "Upside down?"

I nod.

Jake looks at me for more information.

"When that woman, Mary, found us, we were really caught up in her trap. She had a snare set that we didn't see. She cut us down after a short while."

Jake looks thoughtful. "I wonder why she was using a snare. I mean, what did she plan on doing, catch herself a couple of agents?"

"I don't know," I say. "So, where to from here."

Jake gives me a weak smile. "To Garbor of course, though we'll probably have to stop a few times before we get there."

Panvil nods. "Yep, assuming that my calculations are correct, we'll need to stop to get gas at least two times before we get there."

I sigh. Great. Just what I wanted to hear. Every time we stop means more danger.

I lean back in the seat and feel my eyelids droop from lack of sleep. I guess it would be a good time to try to get some sleep. I yawn. I look around to see if anyone else catches it, but no one does.

As I drift off to sleep, I imagine what it will be like once we make it to Garbor. Maybe...just maybe we'll be able to stop running.

Voices. I wake to hear Jake caution Pavil against stopping at an upcoming gas station.

"But why not," Panvil says. "It looks safe to me."

Jake shakes his head. "But it's not. I've been to this area before. It's the only gas station for a hundred miles. I bet it's monitored by agents."

Panvil sighs. "Oh, you're probably right. So what do we do? If we keep driving, we're going to run out of gas."

I look at Jake. He's changed since the last time I saw him. Dang it. We could have passed him off as an agent had he not had to change at that awful camp.

Jake bites down onto his lip. "I have an idea, though it may not work. Panvil, give me that pen that you got from Raftin."

Panvil hands it over to Jake.

Jake writes three sixes on the top of his right hand. "This should do," he says, dark eyes hopeful. He looks up at Panvil. "Give me your right hand."

Panvil looks repulsive. "No way, I don't want to go to hell."

Jake scoffs. "You're not going to go to hell. Really, what else could we possibly do?"

"Prove it," Panvil says. "What proof can you give me that I won't go to hell?"

Jake sighs, annoyed. "You'll only go to hell if it is a tattoo done by an agent. And that is if there really is a hell. I'm not convinced there is."

Frederick, like me, looks ready to chime in. "Oh, I think there is. What with that earthquake the other day and all these end time signs, how could there not be?"

Frederick looks at me for support.

I sigh. I give Jake a steady look. "I might be wrong, but I think there is a hell. And yes, if you take the mark of the beast, that's where they claim you'll go."

Jake gives me a concerned look. "Who claims? The book of Revelation in the Bible? Honestly Kevin, surely you don't believe that. After spending only a little while in Raftin, I came to the conclusion that this is what happened to the other Christians. They were captured and murdered, not Raptured."

I feel my mouth fall open. "Really? You really believe that? As if millions of Christians could wind up dead all at the same time."

Jake looks argumentative. "Well why not? I mean, it makes more sense than saying that all of them were Raptured out."

"No it doesn't," Frederick says. "Kevins right, something supernatural has happened here, or at least that's the way it appears."

Jake chuckles. "The way it appears. Good grief," he says looking between Frederick and me. "You two will believe anything. Just answer me this: how is it possible for anyone to go flying in the sky without an engine?"

He has a good point. Maybe I am crazy to believe in the Rapture. Maybe I am too naïve in my beliefs.

Frederick gives me a knowing look. Then he looks at Jake. "That's just it, isn't it? If we serve a supernatural God, then we can expect him to work in supernatural ways."

Good point. The thing is, I don't know what to believe. Both Jake and Frederick have made good arguments to support their opinions.

Panvil looks ready to say something, but Jake jumps in ahead of him. "Look," Jake says, "it really doesn't matter what each of us believes, we still need to fool the agents."

That's it. I give Jake a superior look, my mind cheering me on. "If you don't believe in the book of Revelation or any of the end time signs, then why didn't you take the mark of the beast when you were imprisoned?"

Jake sighs. "Because...well, I guess because I'm not sure."

"Fair enough," I say, not really wanting to grill Jake.

I extend a hand to him. He looks taken aback.

"Go ahead," I say. "Mark me. It won't matter since it's not the real thing. Plus, I can get rid of it as soon as I want."

Jake looks pleased. He takes my hand and begins to write on it.

Before long, I have three neat sixes etched into my right hand. I stare at it with a degree of apprehension.

I look at Frederick, who lets out a deep sigh. He extends his hand to Jake, who smiles and takes it.

I watch as Jake writes the three sixes on Frederick's hand. From the look on his face, Frederick is by no means any more cheerful to sport a fake mark of the beast than I am.

Jake turns to Panvil. "Well, are you going to let me mark you or not?"

Panvil sighs annoyingly. "Fine, go ahead," he says, offering Jake his hand.

I watch as Panvil nervously looks on, holding the steering wheel with one hand.

"There," Jake says, looking satisfied. "Now we are all marked. Now," says Jake, looking at Panvil, "go ahead and stop at the station coming up."

Panvil nods and then turns in to the parking lot. If Jake is right, then our newly etched hands should be enough evidence to allow us to fill up the tank.

"What are we going to pay with," I say.

Jake turns around and gives me a bizarre look, his dark eyes taking in my face. "What on earth do you mean? Don't you remember that anyone who has taken the mark of the beast can fill up his or her tank for free?"

I narrow my eyes at him. I didn't know that. Again, I'm glad to have Jake back. It's stuff like this that he knows that might just be enough to get us to Garbor.

Panvil pulls up by the gas pumps. Jake gives us one last look of haughty superiority before exiting the car. That's what I like about Jake, he's never afraid.

Immediately, I see an agent come out of the station and greet Jake. Jake shakes his hand and then gestures towards us. I heave a great sigh. I hope this goes well, but something tells me it won't.

"It's official," Jake says to the agent. "We just converted earlier today."

I see the agent looking Jake's hand over. I dare to breathe.

"Just wait a minute," says the agent. He turns around and heads back into the station.

I watch in horror as Jake comes running up to the car and jerks the door open.

"Get moving," he says, climbing into the driver's seat. "It didn't work. If we're lucky, he won't follow us."

Without a question, Panvil nods and then starts the car. He takes off, leaving a trail of dust behind us.

Jake turns around and gives us a fearful look. "The agent said he was going to get a scanner just to be sure."

"What do you mean," I say.

Jake rolls his eyes, clearly upset at how stupid I am. "I mean that that agent was going to scan my mark to see if it's genuine."

"Dang," I say. "That's not good."

Jake looks past me with a fearful glance. "Oh no, that rat's after us. Hit the pedal hard Panvil."

Panvil nods.

I turn around and see a car racing after us. Oh no. Oh dear God help us.

I feel my heart beat quicken as the car behind us gets closer and closer. Something tells me that this isn't going to be good.

"Drive this thing," Jake shouts. "Dang it, they're right on top of us."

Panvil nods several times, looking white. Frederick gives me a worried look.

Jake looks upset. "I said drive this thing," he shouts again.

Panvil presses down on the gas pedal with all his might. I wonder if the engine could blow up. I sure hope it doesn't.

I look behind me at the car, which is now right on our tail. If we escape this, it will be a miracle. Dang, I wish Jake still had that pistol.

"Watch out," Jake shouts. "I think he's going to ram us."

And he does. I lurch forward, my head colliding with the back of Jake's seat. Ouch.

"He's going to hit us again," Jake shouts.

I brace myself this time. The agent's car collides with ours a second later. I lurch forward, my head swimming.

"We're almost out of gas," Panvil says.

Jake gives me a worried look, swallows hard.

I can't believe that my entire getaway is going to end in seconds. I pray to God for help, though I don't know what he could do in a situation like this.

I feel the car dying down, breathing its last breath. I take a deep breath.

"Okay," Jake says as the car begins to barely creep along. "When we stop, don't anyone get out. I might be able to talk us out of this."

Yeah right. Nevertheless, I plan on staying put.

I watch in terror as the agent pulls up beside our car and stops. This isn't going to be good. I just don't see what Jake can do to get us out of this one.

I take a deep breath and prepare for the worst.

I watch in nervous anticipation for Jake to get out, but he doesn't. I hope he has something clever up his sleeves.

"So what do we have here," says the agent. He is a man. He bends down and looks at all of us. Next second, he gives Jake a haughty look. "I knew something was wrong as soon as I saw that mark on your hand. Nice try, but I'm going to have to ask you to come with me."

Jake shakes his head. "Oh no officer, you've got it all wrong. I got my mark from another district, so that's why it looks different."

I wish he wouldn't lie. I look at the agent's car with envy. It looks several years newer than the one I'm sitting in.

"Be that as it may," begins the agent, "all of you are coming with me. So," he says, pulling a pistol from its holster, "shall I fire a shot or two or are you going to come peacefully?"

"Oh, we'll come peacefully," Jake says seriously. "Just put your pistol away and then check our marks just to make sure."

"Fine," says the agent. "I will do exactly that. Only step out of the vehicle with your hands in the air."

Sounds good. Maybe we can take the agent down if we all work together. Oh dear God please help us.

Jake is the first to exit the car. I open my door and slowly step out of the car.

The agent gives us all a haughty look. "If you'll all just line up here," he says, pointing to an area in between the two cars, "then I will check each of your marks."

I half laugh in my mind as I think of saying something stupid like praise be to Vladimir. Vladimir, of course, being the leader of the New World Order.

I look at Jake for guidance, but he isn't looking at me. His eyes are fixated on the agent.

Frederick lines up behind me, and then Panvil behind him. And then a plan begins to take shape in my mind. There are four of us and only one of him. We could take him down.

"Jake," I say hurriedly as the agent gets the scanner out of his car. I see Jake turn his head slightly to listen to me. I decide to step up behind him and whisper in his ear. "If we all worked together, I think we can take him. Go for his pistol, and I will ready my fists."

Jake nods barely visibly.

As the agent heads towards us with his scanner in hand, I can see this whole situation turning around in our favor. If Jake can just get his pistol, then we'll have him.

"Let me see your hand," says the agent. Jake extends his hand towards the agent.

I watch in fear as the agent scans the mark on Jake's hand. And then Jake lunges forward and attempts to grab the agent's pistol from its holster.

The agent growls like a cornered animal as Jake takes hold of the pistol. I flinch as the pistol goes off, stirring up the dust on the ground.

I decide it's time to act. I lunge forward and drive my fist directly into the side of the agent's face. I feel my knuckles collide with his cheek bone. I hate doing this, but there's no other way to get away.

I watch as Jake continues to struggle for the pistol, so I slam my fist into the agent's face a second time. He hollers out and then staggers backward a couple of feet.

I hear a curse word fly out of the agent's mouth as Jake gains control of the pistol. I feel loads better as Jake steps away from the agent, gun in hand.

Jake gives the agent a haughty look. "Now it's your turn to know what it feels like to be hot and thirsty. Get in the car," barks Jake as he aims the pistol at the agent's head.

I watch in jubilation as the agent climbs into our car. Jake slams the door shut behind him.

Jake turns around to face the rest of us. "We'll take his car. It should have more gas than ours. Go ahead and get in," says Jake in a dangerous tone. I'm sure glad he's on our side.

I watch as Jake climbs into the driver's seat. I climb into the back seat and instantly smell the new car smell. The other car smelled like cigarette smoke.

While still aiming the pistol at the agent (the window is rolled down in our old car), Jake starts up the new car and prepares to take flight.

I glance at our old car and watch in horror as the agent opens the door and scrambles to get out of the seat. Jake fires a shot, and I watch as the agent grabs at one of his legs. Jake shot him in the leg.

"He won't get far now," Jake says angrily. "Time to go. Everyone hold on."

Jake slams his foot down on the gas pedal, and we speed away a moment later.

"How much gas do we have," I say.

"Over half a tank," Jake says. He gives me a satisfied look. "You did good back there. I'm not sure I could have done it on my own. But as for the rest of you," Jake says with a frown, "you could have helped."

I look at Frederick, who looks down right irritated to say the least.

"I was going to until Kevin punched him in the face," Frederick says.

Jake turns on Panvil with an irritated expression. "And what's your excuse?"

Panvil looks wounded. "I had a handful of dirt I was about to through in his face when you two jumped in and started working him over."

"Fair enough," Jake says. "It's just as well. You probably would have just got in the way."

I breathe a sigh of relief. "I'm just glad that we made off with a new car and a pistol. That's worth a lot."

Jake nods. "Yeah, it is. I figured that we'd be able to take him. He couldn't have weighed more than a hundred and fifty pounds soak and wet."

I laugh. "Yeah, I saw that."

I watch as the speedometer tops eighty miles an hour. At least this car is able to take the speed. That other car sounded like it was on its last leg.

I lean back in my seat. I yawn. Boy does it feel good to be free again? As soon as that agent pulled up beside us, I felt my freedom dwindle with each passing second. And, had he had a chance to scan all our marks, there is no doubt that he would have tried to capture all of us. I run this by Jake.

"Without a doubt," he says. "He was just looking for an excuse to nail us. Would have hauled us to Raftin I presume if he had had the chance."

"So what now," I say. "I mean, we're all going to need some water sooner or later."

Jake nods. "Yeah, I know. Just wait until we get a little further down the road and maybe we can find a place where there are no agents."

Sounds good to me. But if Jake was right, there won't be any businesses much to speak of for a hundred miles around here. If we can just find some abandoned houses, we might be able to get the supplies we need. I just hope that there aren't any roadblocks up ahead. It'd be just like an agent to try to stop us on the road. These people are determined to mark everyone they can and send the rest to their death.

I watch as the landscape becomes more hilly. Steep hills with rocky outcrops blanket both sides of the road. I hope we happen on some houses sooner than later.

Another thing that I notice about this car is that is has good air conditioning. It was hot riding in the other car. Even with the windows rolled down it was downright uncomfortable.

I take a sharp breath as I begin to see some houses beside the road. Jake, I think to myself, get ready to pull over.

And he does. I watch with a mixture of nervousness and excitement as we pull into the driveway of one of these homes. It looks slightly run down, but not too badly.

Jake gets out of the car a moment later. The rest of us follow suit. I just hope there aren't any agents around here. The place looks peaceful, despite its slightly decrepit state.

Jake walks up to the door and stops. He turns around to face the rest of us. "Be prepared, just in case things don't go well."

I nod.

With his pistol in hand, Jake opens the door and heads inside. I feel my heart pounding a nervous tune in my chest.

I step inside behind Jake. Instantly I notice the smell of decay in the air. Something isn't right here.

Jake presses deeper into the house, his pistol still pointing straight ahead of him. I swallow hard. I hope we can find some food and water.

I walk right into Jake, who has stopped for some reason.

"Oh no," he says warily. "It is as I figured. They are all dead."

CHAPTER 6 The Trap Door

Feeling like I could vomit, I pull my shirt up over my nose and take shallow breaths. I step out from behind Jake and see two bodies lying on the floor and covered with maggots.

"Let's go," Jake says.

I leave the house behind as fast as I can. That was the worst smell I have ever experienced in my entire life. While I am still thirsty, I have no desire to eat anything right now.

After what feels like another hour or so of driving, we begin to pass some other houses. I hope and pray that these houses have no dead or decomposing bodies in them.

"Let's try this one," Jake says, nodding at a nice red brick house. "Maybe we can find what we need in there."

"Maybe," I say warily.

Before we get out of the car, Frederick tells us that he isn't feeling well, so he's going to stay behind. Jake nods and says that that is alright.

We waste no time heading into the house. Jake heads in first, followed by me and then Panvil.

The first thing I notice is the lack of decomposition filling the air. Hopefully, the people who lived here were able to get away safely or were possibly Raptured out.

"Wanna find out," Jake says with a curious half smile. "I'll show you how we can tell if these people left suddenly, as the Rapture portrays, or were taken away by force."

Jake leads us across the spacious living room, which looks like it has just been cleaned recently. Oh no. Someone appears to be living here.

"Take a look at this," Jake says, beckoning us forward. He points to all the dishes in the sink. "Whoever lived here kept a tidy place, but just failed to do the dishes. Oh and look," says Jake, pointing to the kitchen table, "someone left food behind on their plates."

I take a deep breath. "Whoever lived here seemed to have suddenly disappeared."

Jake rolls his eyes. "Not exactly. But it is odd that there are still plates on the table with food on them."

"What could this mean," Panvil says.

Jake looks between Panvil and I. "That whoever lived here left in a hurry."

I don't know why I feel a little irritated at Jake's opinion. I guess it's because I have actually started to believe in the idea of a Rapture.

Jake approaches the cabinets and starts opening them. "Dang, look at all this food. Good Lord, we've struck it rich."

I look at all the boxes of cereal with excitement. I rush over and start opening other doors.

So far, I've found bags of rice and beans, cans of potatoes and several packages of cookies. I haven't seen this much food in months.

Panvil walks over to the sink and turns it on. "We've got water," he says happily.

Dang this is a good place. "Maybe we should just stay here for as long as the food and water hold out."

Panvil gives me a funny look. "That was just what I was thinking. I'll run out and tell Frederick. He'll want to know that we struck it rich."

Feeling extra happy, I pull one of the cups out of the drain rack and fill it full of water.

I take a drink. It is good and cool.

Jake takes a cup and fills it with water as well. After drinking his fill, he sits the cup down on the counter.

While Jake is gathering up all the food he can find, I decided to take a look at the rest of the house. Since there doesn't appear to be anyone home, I think it's a good idea to see what else we can find. Even though Jake didn't want to admit it, I think the people who owned this house could very well have been Raptured out. I mean, the food was still on the plates and everything.

I open up a door and head into what appears to be a sewing room. A big sewing machine is on the other side of the room, surrounded by racks of clothes. I wonder if I can find anything that will fit me.

I see a closet behind one of the racks and decide to see what's in it. I remember the closets in my parent's house were always stacked full of boxes and covered with spider webs. I use to hate taking stuff out of the boxes because there were always spiders crawling on everything.

Nevertheless, I decide to sneak a peek. I open the closet door and find myself staring at a wall of clothes. Well, at least it's not spider infested boxes.

I look through the clothes for any men's, but everything here belongs to a woman.

And then I see it. A small crack on the floor exuding light. I hunker down to investigate.

Oh my gosh. It looks like a...trap door or something. And from the looks of it, someone is down there.

I slowly back away from the closet and head out of the room. I need to tell Jake about this and fast. It looks like the people who own this house are living beneath it.

As I round the corner of the room and head into the hallway, I can hear Jake cursing up a storm. I wish he wouldn't do that. My mom always used to say that everyone will give an account of every word spoken to God.

"What is it," I say, coming into the living room.

"It's the car," Panvil says, looking blown away. "It's gone."

"What," I say, not wanting to believe this.

I run out of the living room and onto the front porch. Panvil was right. Our car is gone. Dang it.

I shake my head and go back inside. "I can't believe he left us," I say, trying not to get too angry. "After all we've done for him and everything."

"Dang it," Jake says, angrily. He runs a hand through his hair, looking distraught. "And just when things started to turn around for us to."

I nod. "Yeah. Oh," I say quickly. "I almost forgot. When I was in the sewing room earlier, I saw a light coming from a trap door in the closet."

Jake looks wild eyed. "You're sure about that."

I nod. "Without a doubt."

"Take me to it," Jake says without another word.

I lead Jake down the hall and into the sewing room. I step lightly so that whoever is down there won't know where right on top of them.

I point to the closet and hold a finger to my lips as a reminder to Jake to be quiet. He nods appreciatively.

With his pistol in hand, Jake bends down to investigate the trap door. Panvil stops at my side, watching Jake.

Very slowly, Jake grabs a hold of the handle on the trap door and opens it. I see a blast of light shoot upwards through the closet. Someone is definitely down there.

I take a step closer, but Jake holds up a hand stopping me.

Jake leans over the opening and says "hello down there. Is there anyone at home."

"Yes," comes a voice from below the opening. "Who are you and what do you want?"

"We're not agents," Jake says. "We're just stopping in on our way to Garbor."

"Come on down then," says the voice.

"Why don't you come on up," Jake says politely.

"I can't," says the voice. "My mother told me to stay here until she got back."

"Okay," Jake says. "I'll come down then."

Jake pushes the pistol beneath the rim of his pants and then starts climbing down the ladder.

"Stay up here for now," Jake says before he disappears into the room below.

I turn to Panvil. "Strange isn't it. Why would a mother leave her boy behind in times like these? Surely she knew that people would come by and snoop."

Panvil shrugs. "Not necessarily. It was hard to find wasn't it."

"Not really," I say.

"Oh," Panvil says. "It's just that I don't think I would have found it."

I can hear Jake down there explaining our situation to the boy.

I listen in as Jake tells the boy about being in Raftin and barely getting away from an agent earlier. It sounds like he's hoping to...

"Who are you," says a voice from behind me. And it wasn't Panvil.

Slowly, I turn around and come face to face with a woman.

I swallow hard. She has a pistol pointing right at my head.

"Please," I say. "Don't shoot. We're not agents or marked people."

"Prove it," says the woman.

I take a deep breath and let it out slowly to try to calm myself. I can't help but stare at the pistol. "We were driving by earlier and decided to stop in for supplies. You see, we were hoping that no one would be at home."

"Well you were wrong," says the woman, dark eyes glinting with fear and suspicion.

I take another deep breath. "Our friend, or who we thought was a friend made off with our car, leaving us stranded."

The woman's eyebrows shoot up. "Oh, he did," she says with disbelief. "And what of your other companions. Why do I hear a man's voice down there talking to my son?"

I swallow. "That is Jake. He's a good person, honestly. He wouldn't hurt a little kid, I promise you."

I watch as the woman pulls back on the gun trigger.

"I'm afraid you're going to have to be more convincing than that," she says. "Otherwise, there's a bullet in this gun with your name on it."

"Let me," Panvil says, drawing the woman's attention away from me. She points the gun at Panvil. "What he said is true. We were just passing by when we decided that this would be a good place to stop. Three of us came inside while one decided to stay in the car. We didn't know anyone was here. From the looks of the place, like the old food on the plates, we were wondering what happened to the people who lived here."

"That's better," says the woman. She looks at us suspiciously. "Let me see your hands."

I decide to let her know what we did before she has a chance to shoot us. I tell her everything, including the car we took from that agent.

She gives me a small smile.

"Look," I say, spitting on my hand. I rub the three sixes off with ease. "You see, this confirms what I told you."

"Well I'll be," she says, bewildered. "So you've been through all of that."

I nod. "And more."

"Tell me your name," she says, demandingly.

"I'm Kevin," I say. I point to Panvil. "And this is Panvil. The third member of our party, Jake, is currently down there talking to your son."

The woman gives us a steady look. "Alright, I'm convinced. Now just what is it that you all need?"

"Food and water for our journey," I say. "If you can spare it."

"I can," says the woman. She extends a hand to me. "Names Melody."

I shake her hand graciously. I breathe a sigh of relief. She lowers the gun and slips it back into its holster.

Melody looks happily between Panvil and me. "Ain't had men folk around here for some time now. If you all are able to earn your keep and supplies, then I'd be obliged to give 'em to you."

"Fair enough," Panvil says. "Just what exactly do you want us to do?"

Melody gives Panvil a serious look. "I've got wood out back that needs to be chopped for this winter for starters. I also need someone to find me some books so my son can read in all his free time. After that, well, I guess I'd be obliged to give you the things you need."

"Thanks," I say, extending a hand to her. "We'll get 'em done."

"Good," Melody says. "Like I said, it's right nice to have some decent men folks around the house in these times."

"About these times," I begin, "what do you think happened to everyone, to all the Christians I mean."

Melody considers this. "Probably rounded up and shot if you ask me. Aint got much to say about it actually. I do know that there's this mark everyone's talking about. My best friend who lives down the road from here got it just this morning, said she could buy and sell now. As for me, well, I'd like to know a little more about what all's been going on before I get the mark. To be honest with you, it kind of scares me a little. I remember some Christians talking years ago that by the taking the mark, you'd lose your soul."

I nod. "Yeah, we've heard the same thing. That's why I don't want to take the mark. That's why none of us have taken the mark."

"So," I begin, "where do you think the best place to look for books are?"

"For my son," Melody says. "Not far down the road from here is an abandoned book store. I haven't had time to go to it myself, but if one of you can go there and get me some books, I'd be mighty obliged."

"I'll do that," Panvil says. He narrows his eyes on Melody. "But how can I get there without a vehicle?"

Melody lets out a scratchy laugh. "You walk that's what you do. I do it every day. Some days I walk six miles into Town just to hear the gossip from some of my friends. Mind you, I am in good shape."

I look at Panvil. "You look like you're in good shape. I bet you can run the whole distance."

Panvil laughs. "I don't know about that, but I could always skip."

I laugh. I look at Melody, who is also laughing, hers high and scratchy.

I walk up to the opening of the trap door. "Hey Jake, we've got company."

I hear Jake let out a string of curse words as he makes his way up the ladder.

As soon as he gets out of the closet, he curses again.

"It's okay," I say. "She's one of us. That was her son you were talking to."

Jake breathes a big sigh of relief. "Good," he says, lowering his pistol.

What I can't figure out is how someone who looks as old as Melody has a son. I decide not to ask. I wouldn't want her to think we were nosy people. Perhaps she adopted before the New World Order took over. I know you can't adopt or have kids now. Anyone who does have kids will have to turn them over to local agents, who then put them to death.

Jake shakes Melody's hand. "I was just talking to your son earlier. Bright lad he is."

Melody looks appreciative. "He is that. Tell me, what do you think about chopping wood?"

I can tell that Jake is quickly catching on. He's just that smart.

"I think it's great exercise," Jake says.

Melody laughs, all pitchy and scratchy. "You sound like my type of man."

I look at Melody. "I have a question for you."

Melody looks ready to answer it. "What's that?"

I swallow. "Well, it's about the food on the plates upstairs. How come you left food on the plates and dishes that haven't been washed yet?"

Melody looks like she might not tell me this. "Well, it's because I want anyone who stops by here to think that we was Raptured out. Not that I necessarily believe in the Rapture, but it looks good. Until I know more about this mark business, I plan to keep to myself mainly."

I nod. I understand. I actually thought about doing the same thing at my parent's house, but there were just too many agents hanging around the area. I don't think it would have worked for me. But out here in this more rural area, I suspect she has a good point.

I look between the three of them. "Well, if you're going to chop the wood and you're going to get the books, what should I do?"

"I can answer that," Melody says. "You can stay here and keep me and my boy company. Get a bite to eat while you're at it. How does that sound?"

I look between Jake and Panvil. "Well, if you two don't mind, that is?"

Even after assuring me that they didn't mind, something told me that they did. They were just too polite to say anything. Jake is a really nice guy. As for Panvil, well, he's nice too, I just don't know him as well. But I do know that he is reliable.

After lowering myself down the ladder and into the cellar, I find myself face to face with a grown boy. He appears to be fourteen or fifteen, and here I thought that Jake was talking to a six-year-old.

I offer him my hand. He shakes it without preamble.

"So," I say, looking around the place, "how long have you two been holding up in this place?"

"Ask a lot of questions don't you," says the boy.

"Sorry," I say quickly.

"Don't be," Melody says. "That's one of the reasons why I suggested you stay here and chat with us. I expected you to ask questions and for us to ask questions in return. As for your first question, well, this is the safest place we had to hold up in. We have an old barn out back, but it's too run down to live in. And, even though this here's a cellar, we've made it mighty comfortable."

"And what about you," says the boy. "Where are you from?"

I swallow. "Well, first off, my name is Kevin. I come from district four, by the ocean. I left home several days ago with the intent on making my way to Garbor."

He snorts a laugh.

Melody looks ready to hit him. "Show some manners boy."

That clears it up quickly. I can see the boy's expression turn instantly.

He gives me a half friendly half irritated look. "My name's Jacob. I'm fifteen years old and was born and raised here in this rugged part of district three."

He talks kind of like his mother. I guess it's from being around her for so long. I have never been around people who have talked like this before.

I nod politely nevertheless. "So, do you ever get out of the house like your mom?"

"Yes," Jacob says. "Just not very often. Mom doesn't want me to get caught by them, agents."

"Yeah," I say. "I don't blame her."

Jacob gives me a funny look. "What kind of talk is that? Where'd you go to school?"

"Lorence High," I say. "It was a fairly good school, although some of the teachers were pretty lousy."

Jacob points a crooked finger at me. "There's the reason. You just didn't get a good education from the sound of it."

I shake my head from side to side. "I guess you could say that. I certainly didn't benefit from having teachers who could barely spell. What about you," I say.

"I was home schooled," Jacob says. "Learned a mighty lot just by doing all the work my mother here made me do. If not for her, well, I don't expect I would have learned much at the public school."

"How come," I say, half wishing I had kept my mouth shut.

Jacob looks slightly embarrassed. "Well, I am dyslexic. I read things differently than most people."

117

I narrow my eyes at him. "That doesn't mean that you wouldn't have excelled in public school."

"Oh yes it does," Jacob says. "Most people don't know what ter do with people like me."

Melody clears her throat, and I can see that she wants me to talk about something else other than school. So I do.

"What about your friends," I say, again wishing that I had brought up something else. This is too closely related to school. Being home schooled, I suspect he didn't have the opportunity to make many friends.

"I have friends," Jacob says coolly. He gives me a dirty look. "Bet you didn't think people like me had many friends did you?"

I swallow hard. "I...didn't know. You don't exactly live in a major Town."

"Good point," Melody says, looking pleased. "Now tell us more about yourself. What were times like before you left home? Were you an only child, that sort of stuff?"

"Sure," I say. I take a deep breath. "Well, I guess it's safe to say that things weren't as good back home as they seem to be here. For instance, nearly two weeks ago when I left, we had agents patrolling the streets and even coming right into our houses. But before that, I have something interesting to say. I woke up one morning to find my parent's gone. I looked everywhere for them in the house and even in Town, but they were nowhere to be seen. Many days went by before I finally decided to leave the area. I heard news about agents lining people up to mark them, and that's when I knew I had to leave."

"Interesting," Melody says. "So did you have very many family and friends disappear?"

I nod. "Yes, nearly everyone I knew. The thing is, I don't recall all of them being Christians. That's what's really been troubling me in the back of my mind."

Melody shrugs. "Maybe many of 'em weren't. I mean, it could be that the people were just all rounded up and sent somewhere, we just don't know where."

"Could be," I say. "I just can't get all this end times stuff off my mind. Stuff like the mark of the beast and the number being his name or whatever. It just seems too much like the Bible. And then there's the earthquake we had the other day. Surely you all felt it, didn't you?"

Melody nods while Jacob appears to be trying to ignore me. "Oh we felt it alright. Look at the wall behind you, it's full of big cracks."

I turn around and look at the wall. Sure enough, several large cracks run from the ceiling to the floor. I turn back around to face Melody.

"It almost swallowed my friends and me up," I say. "It stopped right behind us. When we turned around, there was a huge crack in the ground."

Melody looks at me with her dark beady eyes. "Strange isn't it? It's almost like God if he exists, decided to let you live."

I blink. "Yeah, I guess you could say that."

I wonder how Panvil and Jake are coming along with their chores. I hope that Panvil doesn't meet up with any agents. As for Jake, well, since he is in the backyard here, he'll probably be fine. At least I hope he is. Jake reminds me so much of an older brother I never had.

Melody gives me a friendly look. "What about you? How old are you?"

"Sixteen," I say.

Melody wets her lips. "That's a mighty good age to be. Yes, at that age, you'd likely have more sense than my son here, wouldn't you?"

Surely she doesn't expect me to answer that with him sitting right in front of me. I decide to remain silent.

Melody looks like she forgot something. "I almost forgot. I told you that I'd have food fer ya, didn't I?"

I smile.

Melody raises her eyebrows. "My how you have a mighty handsome smile."

"Mom," Jacob chides. "Leave him alone."

I shrug. "I don't mind." And why would I? It's nice to have a compliment every once in a while.

Melody gets up and makes her way to a small kitchen area. I have to admit, this is a pretty cool cellar. She ruffles some bags and stuff and then puts some food on a plate. I feel myself salivating at the mere thought of food.

"Here," Melody says a moment later. "This ought to make you happy. There's chocolate chip cookies, potato chips, and jelly beans."

I laugh. What a selection. "It sounds great! Thank you."

Melody gives me a warm smile. "I baked the cookies myself," says Melody, looking far away in her thoughts. "Should have enough flour and other ingredients to last us until about this time next year."

"That's good," I say.

I look at Jacob. He doesn't seem to mind that I'm eating him out of house and home.

I take a bite of one of the cookies. "It's good," I say.

Melody smiles. "I knew you'd like 'em. So, if you don't mind, I'd like to tell you a little about myself."

"Sure," I say, popping one of the jelly beans into my mouth. "Yum, blueberry is my favorite."

Melody smiles. "I came to these here parts many decades ago. Not long after I came, I met Jacob's father, who was a coal miner. We quickly married and set out to make our way. This here place is what we were able to buy."

I look at the room around me. "It is a nice place," I say.

"Thank you," Melody says. "Then came a bunch of stupid environmentalists who shut down the coal mines and, well, that just about did us in. We didn't have any income you see. So, I set out to work by growing vegetable and selling them in Town. Made a mighty good amount of money doing that. As for Ben, my husband, well, he found other work eventually, it just didn't pay as much. But, it wasn't nearly as dangerous. He worked in a shoe factory for years, even retired from there. Ever heard of Bowman's Shoes?"

"No," I say.

Melody shrugs. "All well, you were from another district after all. Anyway, we both worked hard for everything we got, even though it weren't much. The thing is, I liked working in the garden, and Ben seemed to like working in the shoe factory. We managed to buy this place. I own it free and clear, although that might change what with this New World Order and everything. Anyway, Ben got to telling me that I was working too much, that I needed to stay at home and school Jacob. So I did. I home schooled him from the time he was five till the time he became a teenager. I taught him a lot. Even taught him how to overcome his reading problem. Well, at least for the most part. And up until recently, we were doing well. And then things started really getting weird. I woke up one morning to find Ben gone. I looked all over for him but couldn't find him anywhere."

I swallow. "Was he a Christian," I say.

"Don't know," Melody says. "Maybe he was maybe he wasn't. I just know that he disappeared like a magician's rabbit. I even had Jacob here search the entire Town for him, but we still couldn't find him. Then came the New World Order, now run by that Vladimir man. I just can't figure out for the life of me what's gotten into this world. Things were going fine, and then, all hell broke loose."

I nod. "I know," I say sadly.

"Anyway," Melody says, "just when our lives were about as good as you could get, all this crap had to come and ruin everything. First it was one thing and then another. I don't know, maybe I'm an old superstitious bat, but I think there's more going on here than we can see. Take my husband's disappearance for example, what could have caused that?"

"I don't know," I say.

Jacob actually looks like he wants to join our conversation. He looks at his mom. "Sure wish we had been Christians, just in case."

So do I. If I had known what all was coming on the earth, I would have converted to Christianity a long time ago. As it is, I'll just have to make the best of it.

I look at Melody. "Are you sure there's nothing I can help you with?"

Melody nods. "Not unless you would care to stack the wood for your friend. If you're really aching to do something, that'd be something good to do."

I rise to my feet. Sounds better than sitting here. Honestly, I feel bad sitting in here eating and relaxing while Jake and Panvil are out working.

I look between Melody and Jacob. "Thanks for the food and conversation. I'd feel better if I went and helped Jake."

Melody smiles. She rises to her feet and walks over to the counter where the food is at. She puts a few chocolate chip cookies into a sandwich bag and then hands it to me. "For your friend."

I take the bag graciously.

After climbing out of the cellar, I walk across the house to the back door. I hope Jake isn't mad at me for not helping him. I open the door and head outside.

"Hey," I say, shutting the door behind me. I give the cookies to Jake. "Melody wanted me to give these to you, they're really good."

"Thanks," Jake says with a small smile. "So, what brings you out here, other than the cookies I mean?

I point to the pile of wood. "I'm going to stack that for starters," I say.

As I begin stacking the wood, I can't help but wonder why Jacob, Melody's son, doesn't do more around here to help her. I guess Melody doesn't want him to for fear of being intercepted by an agent.

I look at the collar of Jake's shirt. It is all sweaty. It is pretty hot out here. I look at the area around me and see an old car sitting in the edge of the woods. I wonder if it still works. There is also an old broken down tractor sitting among a bunch of weeds. I bet Melody used the tractor to work in her garden.

Jake takes a bite out of one of the cookies. "They're good," he says through a mouthful.

I laugh. I like Jake. If I could have ever had an older brother, Jake would have been perfect. He has a good personality, he looks great, and he genuinely cares about other people, a trait becoming scarcer these days.

I glance at the car as I stack another piece of wood. I wonder if the thing would ever start. I run this by Jake.

Jake stops chopping wood for a moment and looks up at me. "What," he says. "Oh, I don't know. Why?"

"Well," I begin, "we could ask Melody if we could use it. You know, maybe work it off or something."

Jake gives me a half smile. "Not a bad idea. If we could get it to start, that is."

I look at the car with high hopes. If we could get this thing started, it might be the perfect ticket to get us to Garbor. In the meantime, I need to finish stacking this wood, so I get back to work. I don't want Jake to feel like he is the only one doing anything around here.

What feels like a couple of hours pass, and Jake and I decide to have a look at the car. From the looks of it, it hasn't been too long since it was driven.

I stop by the driver's side of the car. I bend down and look in the window. It looks clean enough inside. I back away a few steps. As for the outside, it could use a new paint job, but if everything works, that's all that really matters.

Jake opens the door and climbs in. He then starts the car with one leg hanging out of the cab. I hear myself take a sharp intake of breath as the engine starts right up. This is good.

"What about fuel," I say.

Jake wipes some dust off the glass pane to reveal nearly a full tank of gas. Oh my gosh. This would be like the best blessing ever right now if we could use this car.

Jake turns the engine off and climbs out. "Sure sounds good. Let's look at the tires."

Jake and I walk slowly around the car, looking the tires over. While I'm no mechanic, the tires look good to me. It looks like they have plenty of tread left on them.

"This is good," Jake says happily. He gives me a soft punch in the arm. "I think I'll leave it to you to ask Melody if we can take it. She seems to have taken to you the most."

I let out a deep breath. "Really," I say.

Jake nods. "Absolutely."

A couple minutes later, we're back in the room with the secret entrance to the cellar. I lift the trap door and begin my descent down the ladder. Jake waits for me to get at the bottom before coming down.

I meet Melody as soon as I turn away from the ladder. She holds a plate of cookies in her hand.

"Take one," she says, offering the plate to me. "At least one, you've earned it. You see, I snuck a peek at you while you were working. Hardest I've seen anyone work in a long time."

I take a cookie. "Thanks."

Melody smiles. "You're welcome." She turns to Jake, who just got off the ladder. "Ah, and handsome man number two. However, can I thank you?"

Jake ever so slightly raises his eyebrows at me.

I know exactly what he means. The car, of course. I clear my throat. "Melody," I say gently. "We couldn't help but notice as we were working that you have a car at the edge of the woods. Jake and I were just wondering if you plan on using it anytime soon."

Melody blinks. Then she understands. "Oh, yes the car," she says jovially. "Yes, what about it dear?"

I smile. "I was just wondering if you plan on using it anytime soon."

Melody shrugs. "Can't never tell, can you. What with all these strange things going on nowadays, you never know when you're going to need to make a getaway."

I nod. Jake gives me a gentle nod, wanting me to keep trying.

"Well," I say. I take a deep breath.

Melody smiles. "Get it out, boy. You don't have to be afraid of me."

I smile graciously. "Well, you see. We were just wondering if you weren't going to use the car anytime soon...you know, if we could maybe borrow it."

Melody considers this. "Ah, see what you mean now."

Then I have a great idea, a wonderful idea. I look at Melody and decide to do this quickly. "Why don't you and your son come with us? We're headed for Garbor. There'd be plenty of room in that car from the looks of it."

I see a gleam of consideration in her eyes as she considers this. I decided to pray silently. Please dear God, please let her be okay with this.

"Fine," Melody says, shocking me. Honestly, I didn't think she'd go for it. "But I'd need my walking stick along with a number of other provisions. Plus, there's that other friend of yours who should be back here at any time with some books." Melody's eyebrows pull together curiously. "At least I hope he makes it back. A rather dangerous mission I sent him on, but, it's of high importance."

I wet my lips. "We could all go. You know what they say, there's safety in numbers. Plus, we'd all get to talk on the way there."

"Joy," Jacob says, catching me off guard. He gives me a cool look. "First you eat our food, then you want our car. What is it with you?"

Melody turns on Jacob with a sharp look. "Don't say any more. These are good people, I can tell."

"Thanks," I say.

Jake looks like he wants to say something. "You know, if we do this, if we all go together, I think it'd be good for all of us."

Melody nods. "I agree. I think we should set out just as soon as that friend of yours comes back with my son's books. Or, well, at least after we've packed everything we'll need."

I give Jake a big smile. I didn't think it was going to be this easy to get the car. Jake returns my smile with a small nod.

"So," Melody says, rubbing her hands together. "Let's go ahead and start packing up. Oh good Lord, we have a lot of stuff. I guess we'll have to leave most of it behind."

I can't help but feel excited. I...well, I could almost dance right now. I half consider taking Melody's hand and having a go at it, if I didn't think it'd make me look so stupid.

Melody rushes over to the counter of food. "Most importantly is our food. We need to take all of it. Otherwise, the mice will just get it." Melody turns to me. "Help me, my boy. Here," she says, handing me a big plastic bag. "Hold this while I fill it up."

And so I do.

Jake, after asking Melody about some other stuff, begins bagging it up. I look at Jacob, who also appears to be happy. Surprisingly, he looks like he's gotten over his moodiness. I guess he wants to get out of this place more than I thought.

"You know," Melody says, giving me a big smile. "I don't know if there is a God or not, but if there is, I think he sent you to me. After all, it was just going to be a matter of time until an agent found us. As much as I hate to admit it, we couldn't stay pinned up forever without getting out a time or two."

I hear something thump on the floors upstairs.

"Get down," Melody whispers cautiously. "And be quiet."

Melody grabs her gun, which is some kind of rifle and points it to the trap door. Then she looks between Jake and I. "the First person to come through that door that I don't know is gonna be a dead man."

I blink. She's not joking. Wow. What a woman. And I think she could do it.

A minute later and we hear the trap door open. Then a pile of books comes crashing to the floor.

Melody jumps backward, nearly falling over. "Darn you boy," she says. "And here I thought we were being invaded."

Panvil comes down the ladder, muttering something under his breath.

Melody gives her rifle to Jacob, who then sits it down. She shakes her head. "Did you have to just throw 'em down here like that? Good grief, you nearly gave an old woman a heart attack."

Panvil smiles nervously. "Sorry. I dropped a couple upstairs. They are still there. Thought it'd be best to move fast since I think I might have been followed."

Melody suddenly looks ashen faced. "Followed you say. By who?"

"An agent," Panvil says. "He saw me leave the bookstore behind with a supersized handful of books. I hid out in an old building until I didn't see him anymore, then I bolted. Really I'm surprised I wasn't caught."

Melody swallows hard. Then she lets out a deep breath. She looks between Jake and me. "What should we do now? If he's right, then it may be too dangerous to leave right now."

Dang it. And I had hoped that we could get away from here and head for Garbor as soon as possible. It's only going to be a matter of time before there are more and more agents everywhere.

I look up at the ceiling and run a hand through my hair. I lower my eyes to Panvil. "Are you sure? You actually saw the agent?"

Panvil nods. "Yeah, he was across the street from me watching me. I know he was following me that's why I hid for a while."

I shake my head. "And just when everything was coming together so nicely."

Melody pats me on the shoulder. "It'll be alright young man. Just...I don't know, just thank God your friend wasn't caught. That could have been real bad."

"That's true," I say. For some reason, I'm thinking God has more to do in my life than I ever thought possible before. Maybe He does really exist.

As if he knows what I'm thinking, Jake says "I can't help but feel like God is behind wanting us to leave here. I don't know what it is, but something inside me is telling me to leave this place behind as soon as possible."

Jacob rolls his eyes with a snort. He takes a step towards Jake. "Something inside you? Like God talking to you or something?"

126

Jake nods.

"That's stupid," Jacob says. "You're crazy. That's what you are. And full of bull to."

"Jacob," Melody scolds. "Why do you have to be so rude all the time. Good grief," she says, turning back towards Jake. "I taught him better than that."

Jake sighs. "Maybe he's right. Maybe I am crazy. I don't know, it just feels like we need to get moving, that's all."

Panvil runs a hand through his hair. "I agree. The question is, how?"

Then it occurs to me that we haven't yet told Panvil about the car. So, I take a minute and fill him in.

Panvil looks like I felt a few moments ago when I was so happy. "Are you sure though," he says. "That the car can make the journey."

Jake nods. "She started right up for us. Didn't she Kevin."

I nod.

Melody claps her hands together. I'm glad that she isn't mad that we took the liberty of checking out her car.

Melody points to the pile of books and then looks at Jacob. "Pick those up. You're going to be taking all of them with you."

Jacob gives Panvil a cool look as if he wished that Panvil had been unsuccessful.

Melody starts humming a tune. Then she looks up from bagging more food. "You know, I feel so happy right now. I could just kiss you, but I won't. Don't want to seem overly friendly you see."

I laugh. Melody starts humming the tune again. I know I've heard that tune somewhere, I just can't remember the words to it. I decide to ask Melody.

"It's Amazing Grace," Melody says. "I used to sing in the church choir you see, many years ago."

I nod. "I knew I had heard that tune somewhere. Now I remember where. I too used to go to church, though it's been more years than I can count. My mother used to force me to sing, which I hated."

Melody looks taken aback. "But music is so important to a happy life." She turns on Jacob with pursed lips. "I've been trying to get Jacob interested in music, but he just keeps telling me it would be a waste of time since we're not supposed to make much noise down here. Don't want to go attracting any agents you see."

"Of course," Jake says, who is now holding a bag for Melody.

Melody prances around the room, grabbing stuff by the handfuls and packing it away. I laugh. She hears me and throws me a big smile. She seems so happy, so much different than when we first met her.

"Oh praise the Lord," Melody sings. Then she stops and holds a finger to her lips. She suddenly looks like she's remembered something. "I almost forgot. We need to be quiet down here."

I let out a sigh. I thought she heard something upstairs. Good gosh she scared me half to death.

"Now let me see," Melody whispers as she looks around the room. "We've got all the food packed away, along with my mother's best china. Plus we have all of the little things, you know, like gun shells, water bottles, and handkerchiefs."

I don't say anything, but gun shells seem pretty important to me nowadays. Even though I have no plans on shooting anyone, you never know when you'll have to defend yourself. I'm just glad that one of us has a gun.

I pick up a doily and look at it. Melody's eyes widen with a smile.

"I almost forgot to pack them," Melody says gently taking the doily from me. She looks between me and the doily. "My great grandmother made these a long time ago. I would hate to have to leave them behind. You never know if we're coming back here."

I nod.

After another hour or so of packing, Melody puts her hands on her hips and looks around the room with sharp eyes. "Well, boys, that appears to be all we'll be taking with us. I do have more stuff upstairs, but I suppose I can part with it. Lord knows we can't possibly take everything."

"Let's go," Jake says. Jake looks at all the stuff packed up. "It'll take us a few trips to get everything."

Everyone grabs a couple of bags and lines up at the bottom of the ladder. I hope we can make it out of here without getting caught. I didn't like the sound of that agent following Panvil one bit.

I hand Jake my bags once I get to the top of the ladder. Then I climb out of the opening.

Jake hands my bags back to me. "Let's hope and pray that everything goes well."

"Yeah," I say, feeling nervous myself. "Hey, should we get the car and drive around to the front yard, or just leave it where it is?"

"I'd just leave it," Jake says. "It'll give us more cover that way."

I nod.

Over thirty minutes later, we finally have the car packed and ready to go. I was amazed at how smooth everything went. I'm glad that we didn't have any run in with an agent.

Standing by the car, Melody turns around to face her house. "I'm gonna miss you," she says painstakingly. Next second, she turns to face us. "But, I believe we're doing the right thing. Well, we might as well go. Who's driving?"

We all look at each other, trying to figure this out.

"I guess I can," Jake finally says.

Melody nods. "Sounds good to me."

I stand aside to wait and see where Melody will sit before climbing into the car. I don't want to be rude. After all, it is her car. But gosh I'm still irritated at Frederick for leaving us high and dry.

I watch as Melody and Jacob climb into the backseat, leaving me and Panvil standing outside. Panvil gestures for me to ride in the front, which I like. "Thanks," I say.

"No problem," Panvil says. "You and Jake are like brothers. Or, well, at least you look like it."

I climb into the car and shut the door. Jake starts the car and gives me a half smile. I can tell that he is just as happy as I am about getting the car. Melody has proven to be a very generous woman.

"I wish you still had that map," I say, looking at Jake.

"So do I," Jake says. "They took it from me the moment they arrested me back at camp."

"Did someone say map," Melody says from the backseat.

I turn around to face her. "Yeah, Jake use to have a map before an agent took it away from him."

Melody gives me a big toothy smile. "No problem there," she says, excited. I watch as she opens her purse and pulls out a map. "Here," she says, handing it to me.

"Thanks," I say, taking the map. I look it over to find it has a few small holes on the edges like a mouse has chewed on it. Nevertheless, it is much better than nothing.

"Here," I say, handing the map to Jake.

Jake takes the map with a smile. "Let's see," he says, looking the map over. He points to a spot out in the middle of nowhere. "I'd say we are right about here."

Jake unfolds the map to reveal more of the country. He points to a place that appears to be hundreds of miles away. "There is where Garbor is supposed to be." He looks up and gives me a serious look. "Let's hope and pray that we make it."

I nod.

Jake lays the map on the dash and looks in the rearview mirror. "Are you all good back there? Nothing else you need from the house?"

Melody shakes her head. "Nothing that I can't do without. I suspect I'll make at least one agent happy when he comes a snooping. There's enough stuff left in the house to furnish a small castle."

I laugh. "That there is."

Melody digs into her purse. She pulls out a small bag and offers it to me. "Piece of candy?"

"Um, sure," I say, caught off guard.

I take a piece of butterscotch candy and unwrap it. I pop it into my mouth. "It's good," I say.

I take a piece for Jake. Jake thanks, Melody and then pops it into his mouth.

"Away we go, away we goooooo," Melody sings. "Hope you all don't mind me singing from time to time."

"I don't care," I say, not bothering to turn around. I look at Jake. He returns my look with a funny smile.

Jake looks in the rearview mirror. "Well, if everyone is set, then we can go."

"I'm fine," Panvil says.

"There won't be no going back, at least for a while," Jake says.

Melody nods. "I know. I understand that. When you're ready, then we are."

Jake nods with a smile. "Then let's go."

CHAPTER 7 The Final Hurdle

I watch as Jake presses his foot down on the accelerator. Very slowly, the car moves away from the edge of the woods. Oh please dear God let this work.

Jake gives me a quick sideways look. "So far so good."

"Yeah," I say, thankful.

Melody clears her throat a little, getting at least my attention. "I've had this old car for over a decade now, and it hasn't failed me yet. Sure it's had to have a few small things done to it, but thankfully nothing major."

"The tires look good," Jake says.

Melody looks at Jake's side profile. "That's because I had new ones put on not a year ago. I told the mechanic to find me some nice used tires that still had lots of tread."

Jake slows down as he meets the highway. I sure hope that there aren't any agents around.

Jake looks back and forth, down both sides of the road. "Which way," he says, grabbing the map.

"Take a right," Melody says. "And don't worry about using the map just yet. I know my way around these parts better than an agent."

That's good.

Jake follows Melody's advice and turns right. I watch the area for any sign of agents. So far so good.

"You know," Melody begins, "I haven't had this much excitement since my husband was alive. I reckon he'd be right proud that we're making good use of his car."

"Oh," I say. "The car was his?"

Melody nods. "Yep, he bought it just to run around Town in. Up until a couple of months ago, we had two cars. Then along came the agents. It didn't take 'em no time to find ways to swindle us out of some of our property. They claimed that a law had been passed limiting car ownership to everyone. So, he took our other car. In a way, I was glad because this one was my husband's. But I reckon that if it had been in the front driveway instead of the other one, they would have taken it instead."

I frown. "I didn't know that about cars, the limitation of ownership, I mean."

Melody nods runs a hand through her salt and pepper hair. "Oh yes. I'm surprised you didn't know about it. After they took our car, they came and took the best tractor that we had. That really made me angry. Didn't even offer to pay us anything for it." Melody shakes her head. "I'll tell you what, these are not good people, these ones that have taken over."

"I know," I say. I turn around to face Melody. She sits in the center of the backseat. "That's why I decided to leave home. I left everything behind in order to make a quick getaway. Well, I didn't have much to leave behind. My family was fairly poor."

Melody gives me a small smile. "Ain't no shame in that. I came from a poor family. For years I didn't have nothing to eat but beans and cornbread. Then I got married, and everything changed for the best. With my husband and me both earning, we were able to accumulate a few things."

"That's good," I say, still facing Melody. "But it seems like country folk has always had more than city folk."

Melody considers this. "Just depends on the way you look at it. Take homes in big Town's for instance, they're worth as much or more than my house, land, and car combined in some cases. Just depends on where you live."

I look at Panvil. "What about you? Where are you from?"

"The city," Panvil says.

I swallow with nervous excitement. "Do you mean *the* city? Or just a big Town?"

"Oh I meant *the* city of course," Panvil says. "Lived there my whole life."

I've never been to Urichland, but I've always wanted to. It is the only place in the entire country that is called a city and not a Town. And from what I've heard, it has over sixteen million people living in it.

"What was it like," I say.

"Loud," Panvil says. "And noisy and crowded. I left there a few weeks ago just as soon as I heard of the creation of the New World Order. From what I heard, Urichland was going to be the first place in the country to adopt a completely different set of laws. So, instead of sticking around to watch people lose their heads, I decided to leave."

133

Jake laughs. "Sounds like my story."

I look at Jake. "What is your story?" Honestly, I'm more interested in Jake's story than any of the others. I seem to have more in common with him than any of the others.

"Oh nothing much," Jake begins. "I was going to leave my Town even if the New World Order hadn't been established. I wanted to travel, you see. I wanted to see the world."

"How much of it did you get to see," I say.

Jake looks at me out of the corner of his eye. "Not much. I left home three days before me, Leslie, and Donna found you holding up in that tree."

"Really," I say, finding that hard to believe.

Jake nods. "Yep. As soon as I heard of the New World Order, I knew there'd be problems. That's why I thought it best to leave everything behind and set out to find a safe place. We were on our way to Garbor when we found you in that tree."

"What tree," Melody says from the backseat.

I turn around to face her. "Oh, I forgot to tell you. Jake and his friends found me not long after I left home. I was hiding in a tree one night when they found me."

Melody laughs. "What kind of tree? Well, never mind, I don't guess that matters."

"It was a big oak," Jake says, coming to a stop. He looks in the rearview mirror for directions.

"Turn left here," Melody says. "Before long, you'll cross over railroad tracks, then you'll want to take a right. That'll take you west."

"Sounds good," Jake says.

Before long, I find myself struggling to stay awake. I look at the sun. It is about to set. For some reason, I feel really groggy. I run this by Jake. I hope I'm not getting sick.

"You're probably just tired," he says. "Go ahead and sleep. I'll wake you if anything happens."

I nod. And, before I can say anything else, I can feel sleep pulling me under, like an anesthetic.

Bright colors of yellow, orange, and red flash behind my eyelids. I see several big piles of leaves in the front yard. I look up. My mother is walking across the lawn towards me. She looks impressed.

"Great job," she says with a smile. "I figured it'd take you a lot longer than this. Lord knows no one likes to rake leaves, but it has to be done."

I roll my eyes. I get sick and tired of my mom referring to a Lord. It is like she is bound and determined to shove this religious stuff right down my throat.

Mom purses her lips gives me a knowing look. "You know, you may not like it, but you need to hear it. God is going to come back one day, and I want you to be prepared."

I laugh. I lean on my rake as I look up in the sky. I half consider dropping the rake and throwing my hands up in the sky to shout praises to God. That'd sure make my mom think twice about bringing up religion.

Mom sighs. "Fine. As usual, you look like you don't want to hear a word I say. Just remember this: God will be there for you when you need him, and you will need him at some point. Just you remember that."

I open my eyes to find Jake pulled over and looking at the map. I yawn. I needed that nap. "Aren't lost are we?"

Jake looks up from the map and meets my eyes. "I don't think so, were just a ways beyond the territory that Melody is familiar with."

"Oh," I say, feeling some better.

I turn around to look at the backseat. Everyone but Melody appears to be asleep. I watch as Panvil's chest rises and falls with every breath.

"Have a good nap," Melody says.

I nod. "Yeah, I needed it."

"Okay," says Jake. I turn back around to face him.

Jake points to a spot on the map. "I'd say that we are somewhere right in this area if I'm right. So, from the looks of it, we are a lot closer to Garbor than I thought."

I swallow. "Wow," I say, looking at the map. Jake holds a flashlight over it, illuminating everything with a yellowish orange light. "That's great!"

"That's what I told him," Melody says from the backseat. "Won't be too long now. Still, we'll have to stop and get some gas at some point."

I feel my happiness shrivel. Just what I wanted to hear. It seems like we're always one gallon away from walking. I run this by Jake.

Jake laughs. "That's a good one, 'one gallon away from walking.' But I guess it's the truth. Melody's right, we're going to have to find some fuel and quick. This car uses more fuel for some reason."

"Because it has a big engine," Jacob pipes up from the backseat. "Don't you know anything about cars?"

"Jacob," Melody chides. "Show some respect to your elders."

"Sorry," Jacob says, barely audible.

Jake puts the map up and then grips the steering wheel with both hands. I say a quiet prayer inwardly. I wish I didn't worry so much about what others think of me, but I've always been this way.

Jake puts the car in gear and then sets off. I look up at the sky. I can see a hint of light on the horizon. Dawn is right around the corner. I hope we can make it to a gas station soon. I lean back in the seat and try to relax. So far we haven't seen any sign of an agent. I hope it stays that way.

Nearly an hour rolls by and we see no sign of a gas station yet. I feel a twinge of panic in my chest. This isn't good. All we need right now is to have to walk the rest of the way to Garbor. That'd make life miserable for us.

Jake gives me a solemn look. I can tell what he means without saying a word. If we can't find fuel fast, then we'll all be walking. And that puts us at a great risk for other problems. Plus, we'd likely have to leave some of our stuff behind. Everything would be too much to have to carry.

I hear Melody praying in the backseat. I guess that's a good idea. The thing is, I didn't think she was very religious.

"There," Jake says. "What's that coming up? It looks like a gas station."

"I think it is," I say. I breathe a sigh of relief.

Jake turns into the parking lot and drives up to the fuel pump. The thing is, I don't think any of us have any money. Plus, none of us carry the mark of the beast, which you have to have in order to buy or sell.

"What if there are agents," I say.

Jake sighs. "It's a risk we have to take."

I watch as an old man comes hobbling out on a cane to meet us. Jake gets out of the car and walks around to talk to him. So far so good.

I can hear Jake asking the man how he's doing. Jake is exceptionally polite. I hear the man ask to see his mark, which doesn't surprise me. I hear the man tell Jake to leave in a loud voice. I take a deep breath. Jake needs help. I decide to get out and see what I can do before it's too late.

I open the door and climb out of the car. I see the old man give me a sharp stare. Not a glare, but not too far off.

I walk up to the man and extend a hand. Unfortunately, he doesn't shake it, so I lower it to my side.

"Good morning," I say in a happy voice. "I guess my friend here told you that we're in need of gas."

The man gives me a nasty look. "And there'll be none given. The law forbids me from doing business with the likes of you. If I were you, I'd find the nearest Town and then locate the Compound where you can get the mark. Otherwise, you all are going to be tracked down and charged with high treason. At that point, you won't be given a choice to take the mark, you'll lose your head."

I let out a sigh. "Maybe so, but none of us knows where the nearest Compound is. And even if we did, there's no telling what kind of treatment we'd get from a bunch of agents. Take my friend here for example. He was arrested and put into one of the Compounds not far from here. Just because he didn't have the mark, he was treated badly. So you see, we want to try to make it as long as we can without taking the mark. And then there's that part where you could lose your soul."

The old man snorts a nasty laugh. "Lose your soul. You mean to tell me that you believe in the hogwash?"

I shrug. "Don't know for sure, but it's better to be safe than sorry."

"What do you have to offer in exchange for fuel," says the old man.

I swallow. Without a second thought, I say, "a solid gold pocket watch."

The old man's eyebrows shoot up. "Really, can I see it?"

I reach down into my pocket. It's gone. Of course, it must have fallen out when I was jerked upside down the other day. Dang it.

"It's gone," I say, deciding to tell the truth. "I lost it."

The old man laughs sarcastically. "Well, in that case, beat it. And if I see you all around here again, I'll turn you in myself."

"Wait," says a voice from behind me.

It is Melody.

Melody takes off her watch and hands it to the man. "It's gold. And then there is this," she says, reaching into her pocket. She hands the man a coin. "And that there's solid gold."

The old man looks at the coin with piercing eyes. I can tell that he is checking for its authenticity. He must know something about coins. He holds the coin up towards the sky and looks at it.

The old man lowers his gaze from the coin to Melody. "Fine," he says. "A half a tank of gas for these here trinkets."

Melody's mouth falls open, taken aback. "But that stuff is worth more than several tanks of gas."

The old man gives her a nasty smile. "Either take the deal or leave."

I give Melody a desperate look. I want her to take the deal. A half a tank of gas would get us a long ways.

"Deal," Melody says, extending a hand to the man.

Surprisingly, the old man shakes on it.

After getting a half of a tank's worth of gas, we set out again for what I hope is the last leg of our journey. The sun has risen high enough in the sky to illuminate everything with an early morning light.

I look at the red sky. I think of the old saying that goes with it. Red sky at night, sailors delight, red sky in morning, sailors take warning. I laugh. Other than a pinkish red sky, everything looks normal to me.

"Look at that," Jake says, getting my attention.

I look at him with raised eyebrows. I follow his finger to the sky ahead of us.

"It looks...it looks like the sky is bleeding," Jake says. "I've never seen anything like it before."

"Good Lord," Melody says from the backseat. "That is weird."

I can feel the car slowing down. I watch as a blanket of red begins to cover the sky. It's so weird. Must be a storm. I swallow hard. No, I've never seen a storm like this before. Before long, the entire sky is covered with a thick mass of red, hiding the sun.

"This is weird," Jake says. "Must be a different weather pattern around here than back home."

"Yeah," Panvil says from the backseat. "That's probably what it is. I've heard about the strange weather in these parts before."

I blink and then see a drop of something red land on the windshield. This catches Jake's attention to.

I watch as several drops of the mysterious red liquid stick to the windshield. Pretty soon, it is raining red drops.

"I've heard about this before," Jake says. "It happens when a storm sucks up dirt from the ground and then mixes with water." He grabs the map as he slowly drives along. "Yep, just like I thought. We're in the area of what was known as Kansas in the Old Country."

I watch as dozens of drops begin falling on the windshield. If this is dirt, it's the weirdest dirt I've ever seen.

Jake nods toward the sky. "Must be a strong storm, because this stuff's thick."

"That's not dirt or mud," Melody says from the backseat. "Look at how thick it is. No, that's blood."

"Blood," says me and Jake at the same time.

I turn around and give Melody an incredulous look.

"I'm serious," Melody says. "It's one of the things that's supposed to happen during the Great Tribulation. I remember reading it. And the rain became blood or something like that." Melody looks thoughtful. "No, that can't be right. In the Bible, there were hailstones that fell with the blood."

Before long, the entire windshield is covered with red mud. I can't believe that Melody thinks it's blood. That's ridiculous.

I flinch as I hear something pounding on the roof above us. It sounded like...no, it can't be hail.

I turn around and look at Melody. She gives me a knowing look.

Pretty soon, several hailstones start pounding the car.

"I can't see," Jake says, coming to a stop. "I don't want to run off the road."

And then it happens. Thousands of hailstones begin to pound the car. I scrunch my face up as the sound is deafening.

I watch in fear as the mud thickens. I can't see out any of the windows now.

I wish it'd stop hailing. The hailstones don't seem to be very big, there's just so many of them.

"Look at how red that is," Melody says, leaning forward and pointing. "That's blood you all. We need to get out of here and fast."

"We can't," Jake says. "I can't see through the windshield."

"We're stuck," I say, confirming my worst fears.

As the sound of the hail begins to lesson, I have hopes that it is soon to be over. This is crazy. Whoever heard of it raining thick red mud and hailstones?

Jake tries to use the windshield wipers, but they won't work. From the looks of it, there is at least two or three inches of mud that needs to be removed from the windshield.

Once the sound of the hail and rain have stopped, Jake opens the door to the car. "Oh my gosh," he says, sounding like someone was murdered. He looks at me and motions me to open my door. So I do.

I come face to face with what looks like a foreign planet. The entire ground is covered in thick red mud. Even the hailstones are covered up.

I lean over and wipe a finger across the ground. It's warm and sticky. I rub my fingers together. It's so strange.

"It's blood," Melody says again.

"Impossible," Jacob says. Panvil says the same thing.

"Open the door," Melody says to Jacob.

Jacob opens the door and gets out. I hear him yell as he slips and falls to the ground.

Melody leans over and runs a finger across the thick stuff. "It is blood. Blood and hail."

I swallow hard. I say nothing. It is blood, or at least that's what it looks like.

I watch as Jake sticks the tip of a red finger into his mouth. And then I see the expression on his face instantly change to a very serious one. "It's blood," he says. "Okay, now I'm a believer. The church was Raptured out the other day. This must be part of the Great Tribulation."

"I...can't believe it," I say. "How can this be possible?"

Jake looks between me and his bloody fingers. "There's only one explanation for this. There is a God."

I swallow hard. So it's all true. I mean, all of the end time prophecies. I shake my head inwardly. I just can't believe this is happening.

"Oh it's blood alright," Panvil says.

I turn around and watch as Panvil rubs one of his thumbs and index fingers together. "I just don't believe it. How can this be possible? I just...can't believe it."

I pinch myself just in case I'm dreaming. Ouch, I say inwardly. No, this is definitely not a dream.

Jake slowly gets out of the car. I watch in fear as he holds on to the car door for support. He leans over and wipes a hand down the windshield. I watch in astonishment as thick blood slides down to take the place of that that Jake just wiped off.

This is real. This is really happening. But if this is really blood, then that means that there are several more plagues yet to follow.

"Oh my gosh," I hear myself say. "I missed the Rapture."

"We all did," Melody says from the backseat.

Jake slips and nearly falls to the ground. "Dang it's slick. I don't imagine that the car would even go on this stuff."

"So what do we do," I say, worried.

"We wait," Jake says, climbing back into the driver's seat. "We wait until it dries. That's all we *can* do."

"But who knows how long that could take," Jacob says.

"Exactly," Panvil says.

"We're stuck," I say, not wanting to believe it.

Hours roll by, and each time Jake gets out to check how slippery it is, he always ends up coming back with a bad report.

So, I watch with no small amount of anxiety as Jake get's out again to test the ground. And, while we can't go anywhere right now, I figure that any agents caught out in this stuff are experiencing the same thing.

I think of the story in the Bible, where Noah sent out the dove to check for any dry ground. Jake, our dove, leaves the door behind and moves towards the front of the car.

Jake runs a hand down the windshield, wiping the blood away. I'm surprised at how easily it is going away. It's like gel, partly dried and partly moist.

After wiping off enough blood for both of us to see out the windshield, Jake climbs back into the car. "That'll have to do," he says. "What we need is a good rain, a good old fashioned hard rain to wash it all off."

I swallow. Jake starts the car, and I watch in amazement as we begin to move.

"Oh no," I say. "I can't see the markings on the road. How are we going to know where the road is?"

Jake sighs. "We'll just have to do the best we can. I have a pretty good idea. Look at the slope on the sides of the road. Anywhere between there is the road. So, as long as we stay in between the sloped areas, we should be fine."

I nod. "It feels like cotton," I say.

"What," Jake says with a frown.

"Cotton," I say. "It reminds me of driving over cotton."

"Interesting," Jake says in a serious voice.

Very slowly, we press onwards towards Garbor. I still can't believe this has happened. It's like everything that I remember hearing about the Bible is flooding my mind right now. If the Rapture really happened, and this is the Great Tribulation, then that means that Jesus is real too. Oh my gosh."

And then something strange begins to happen. Small drops of rain begin falling onto the windshield. I shake my head inwardly. I can't believe that I now see regular rain as strange.

I watch in amazement as the rain mixes with the blood and runs down the windshield in rivulets.

In my mind's eye, I see an image of the Red Sea parting and allowing the children of Israel to walk through on dry ground. This blood and hail mean that that story really happened. If we are really in the Great Tribulation, then everything that was recorded in the Bible really happened.

The rain really begins to pick up in intensity. Streams of bloody water run down the windows, each stream confirming the times we're living in.

"Look," Jake says, nodding ahead. "You can see part of the highway now."

And so you can. Oh, thank God. I'm a believer now.

I look at all the blood as we drive by. Streams of bloody water now roll beside the highway. It looks like all of the hail has melted. I'm just glad that the hail didn't break our windshield because it was really coming down there for a while.

After another hour or so of driving, the rain clouds begin to break up, allowing the sun to shine through holes in the clouds.

And then I see something strange way up ahead. "What is that," I say.

"Mountains," Jake says. "We're a lot closer than I thought."

I thank God inwardly. Since we are still heading west, then that must be the Rocky Mountains. I feel my breath hinge in my throat. Garbor is said to be somewhere in the Rocky Mountains. We must be very close.

"Don't let that fool you," Jake says.

"What do you mean," I say, looking at him.

"The mountains," he says. "They're still a long ways off. I always heard that you could see them a long time before you actually get there."

Great. Just what I wanted to hear. In that case, I might as well go to sleep. Maybe when I wake, there'll be some good news to share.

I wake to Jake talking to Melody. It sounds like they're discussing fuel again. Just what I wanted to hear. I look at the fuel gauge. We're almost on empty. I look up. The mountains are still a long ways off. Oh good Lord.

I hold my breath as the car begins to cough. Again, just what I wanted to hear. I feel a twinge of panic as the car stalls on the highway. I look at the highway. At least there's hardly any blood left. It looks like most of it got washed away.

"Great," Jake says with a sigh.

"Now what," I say.

"We wait," Jake says. "Maybe someone will come by and give us a ride."

I swallow hard. "But we're out in the middle of nowhere."

"I know," Jake says a little hotly. "But it's either that or walk." I wish we had gotten a full tank of gas instead of just half of a tank.

Hours roll by without a person in sight. This isn't good. Plus, it's not exactly cool outside. I expect it's near a hundred degrees. We roll the windows down manually to let some air in.

Jake gives me a serious look. "I think it's time to walk," he says. "Otherwise, we're just sitting ducks for an agent."

"I agree," Melody says. "But let's just take the food. After what we just experienced, none of that other stuff means that much to me right now."

It's strange how something can change your entire outlook on life within such a short period of time.

Jake opens the door and gets out. I follow suit.

Dried blood crunches beneath my shoes. I am reminded of the time in the Bible when God turned all the water in Egypt to blood. Jeeze, it really did happen. All of that stuff that my mom used to try to convince me was true is true.

As soon as Melody gets out of the car, she stretches and yawns. I catch it.

We all walk around to the trunk of the car. Jake tells us to grab just the important stuff, being the food, water, and a few other basic necessities like matches.

After gathering up all our supplies, we set out towards the mountains. It feels good to stretch my legs. I just wish that we didn't have to run out of gas to do it.

"How far," I say, getting Jake's attention. "How far do you think we'll have to go?"

"Hard to say," Jake says. "Maybe two maybe three hundred miles. I don't know for sure. I just remember hearing that Garbor was nestled somewhere within the Rocky Mountains, that's all."

Great.

"Look," Melody says behind me.

I turn around and see her pointing to a very bright rainbow in the sky. I swallow hard. It said in the Bible that rainbows are signs from God. Wow. God *is* real.

We strike off towards the mountains, bags of supplies in hand. Every once in a while I think I hear someone coming, and I have to turn around and sneak a peek. It'd be our luck to be arrested by an agent out here. The thing is, we can't get off the road. Otherwise, we eliminate our chance of being picked up by a good person. Surely there are a few good people left in the world that would give us a ride.

I would ask Melody what time it is, but I just remembered that she traded her wrist watch, along with the gold coin, for fuel. So much for that. Nevertheless, it feels like we've been walking for hours. My feet hurt and my legs are beginning to feel numb.

"Listen," Jake says, coming to a stop. He turns around to face the road behind us. "Someone's coming."

I look down the road and listen, but cannot hear anything.

And then all of a sudden, I hear it. Someone is coming.

We get off the road and stand at its side. Jake tells everyone to get out their valuables to flash as the person drives by. Maybe, just maybe we can get a ride then.

I watch in nervous excitement as an old school bus comes down the road towards us. It is faded yellow and coming up fast.

Jake tells us to get ready to flash our stuff. The thing is, the only stuff we have to flash is a little food, water, and an old necklace that belongs to Melody.

"Okay, flash it," Jake says.

We all wave our stuff in the air, making me feel a bit stupid really, but what else can we do? We've just got to get on that bus, we've just got to.

I watch as the bus drives by, leaving tracks in the dried blood.

"It's gone," I say, hardly believing my ears.

I swallow hard. I look between Jake and Melody. "Now what?"

"Look," Panvil says excitedly. "The bus, I think it's backing up."

"It is," Jacob says happily.

Sure enough, the bus is backing up. It backs all the way up to us, and then stops.

"Hey there," says a familiar voice.

Oh dear God.

"Can you all believe it," says the old man from the gas station. "We really are living in the Great Tribulation. This *is* really hell on earth."

Jake nods. "Can you give us a ride? We have supplies we can give you."

"Sure," says the old man. "Get on board."

I can hardly believe my ears. That mean old man who was so nasty to us earlier is actually offering us a ride? I can't believe it.

Without another word, we all take turns getting on the bus. What I want to know is how he came to own an old school bus.

"Just sit wherever you can," says the old man. I can see why. He has half the bus filled with boxes of odd and end stuff.

I thank the man as I walk by.

"You're very welcome my boy," says the old man, surprising me. "Isn't this an amazing time to be in? Isn't this an amazing time to live in? Who would have known that I'd live to see the Great Tribulation? Or that any of us would?"

I sit down behind the driver's seat and put my two bags of supplies in the floor between my feet.

Jake sits down beside me. Melody and Jacob sit right across from us, while Panvil sits behind us. Overall, we couldn't ask for better accommodations.

I bet this bus uses a lot of fuel. I stand up and look over the seat at the fuel gauge. Looks like we've got a full tank. That's good.

"Need something," says the old man.

I shake my head no.

"Well if you do, just let me know," he says. "My name's Clifford by the way."

"I'm Kevin," I say, not worrying about giving my name out to him.

"Nice to meet you," Clifford says. "And don't worry about our destination, I know the way."

I feel taken aback. "You do."

Clifford nods. "Yep, I helped build the place. Garbor is only about fifty miles into the Rocky Mountains. Don't you worry about a thing, I'll get us there."

Well, that's nice. I look at Jake. He gives me a small smile with slightly raised eyebrows.

I clear my throat, prepare to talk. I lean forward in my seat so that Clifford can hear me. "How long ago has it been since you were at Garbor?"

"About six months," Clifford says. "We started building it over ten years ago. Thought this day might come, you see."

I frown. "But if you thought this day might come, why weren't you prepared for the Rapture?"

"I thought I was," Clifford says. "Until my wife disappeared. That's when I knew that something strange had happened. I just didn't know it was the Rapture until that blood rain."

"Oh," I say. "So you're sure that Garbor is only fifty miles into the Rocky Mountains."

Clifford gives me a thumbs up. "Yes, unless they moved it, which I doubt they have. It took too long to build, so I doubt they moved it anywhere else."

Well, that's a relief. I look at Jake. He gives me a sleepy look.

"Hey," I say, getting Clifford's attention. "You wouldn't mind if we slept for a while, would you? We've been on the go for so long, we're all pretty tired."

Clifford shakes his head. "Go right ahead. I don't need anyone to help me find Garbor anyway."

"Thanks," I say with a yawn. For too long I've been living on very small naps. I know that I'm running a serious sleep deprivation.

I give Jake one last look and then close my eyes. I feel sleep pulling me under. I could use several hours, although I probably won't get it. My luck, there'll be a bump in the road or something else.

I see a long line of traffic up ahead. I wonder what's going on. I look at the fuel gauge. I hope we don't run out of gas.

As we get closer to the traffic, I can see a man standing in the middle of the road stopping people. Jake tells me to drive slower, but I want to turn around and go a different direction.

There are three cars ahead of me, waiting to be stopped. I feel a twinge of nervousness in my chest. I hope there isn't a problem.

Now it's our turn. I roll down the window and see a middle aged agent walk up to our car.

"Show your mark," barks the agent.

I just look at him like I'm stupid. I don't have a mark. What should I do?

I decide to tell the truth. I wish I had some way of getting away from this man. Nevertheless, I say, "I don't have a mark."

I swallow hard as the agent gives me a hateful glare.

"Get out of the car," he says.

I stay put. "No," I say. Instead, I decided to make a run for it.

I back up a little bit and then turn sharply. I drive off the highway and out into the adjacent field.

"What are you doing," Jake shouts. "That was an agent back there. Do you know what the price is for disobeying an agent?"

"I don't care," I say loudly. "I'm not going to die."

So I drive as fast as the bumpy ground will let me. I head away from the highway. I see the mountains coming up fast. If I can just get to the mountains, I'll be safe.

"They're right behind us," Jake shouts. "We can't outrun them."

"We have to try," I shout. I look at the speedometer. We're going ninety miles an hour. I hope the engine doesn't blow up.

As I race towards the mountains, I pray silently to God for help. Jake is right, the agents following us must have better vehicles.

"We're nearly there," I say.

"Whoa," Jake shouts, scaring me half to death. "Look," he says, pointing to the mountains. "Where'd they go?"

That's a good question. The mountains are gone. Great. I remember reading something like this happening in the Bible. This isn't good.

"They're right on top of us," Jake shouts, getting on my nerves. I wish he'd stop shouting. "Go faster."

"I can't," I say. "The car sounds like it's about to blow up already."

I look at the ground ahead and slam on my breaks. Oh no, it's too late.

I shout at Jake for help as we drive off into a huge hole.

I wake with a jerk.

Jake gives me a knowing look. "Bad dream?"

I nod. "Yeah, we were being chased by agents. And then I drove off into a big hole where the mountains used to be."

"Sounds scary," Jake says.

"Yeah," I say. "It was. How long was I asleep?"

"A couple hours," Jake says.

I let out a deep breath. All well, a couple hours is better than nothing.

"Hey," I say, leaning forward in my seat. "We're nearly there."

"Yep," Clifford says. "Only a couple more hours by my estimates. Then we'll have it made in the shade."

I laugh. "Sounds good," I say.

I turn around to tell Melody the good news. But she is asleep. I'm not going to wake her. I'll let it be a surprise for her.

I lean back in my seat and enjoy the ride. This is actually more comfortable than riding in Melody's car. Of course, I'm not going to tell her that. I wouldn't want her to think me ungrateful. After all, we made it a long ways in Melody's car.

Jake and I spend the next several minutes talking about Garbor. He said that he heard it has a high powered electric fence around it to keep out agents and other troublemakers. This sounds good to me. He also said that everyone has to work, in order to keep the place going. Some of the jobs he mentioned are farming, logging, and cooking. I'm not sure what I'd be good at doing. I've never done any of them.

"Welcome folks to the Rocky Mountains," Clifford says.

I turn around and see Melody just waking up. I give her a polite smile and then look out my window. Jeeze these mountains are big.

"Not far now," Clifford says.

Jake smiles and then leans forward to see out our window. "Looks good," he says. "If we can just get there without having any problems."

I nod. "Yeah, that'd be good."

I turn around to face Melody. "You did bring your gun with you didn't you?"

Melody nods. "Yes, it's in the seat behind me."

"Good," I say. "Not that I like guns, but you just never know when we'll need one."

"I know," Jake says. "I had a chance to shoot the agent who arrested me, but I chose not to. I didn't want to hurt him."

I give him a sad look. "So they confiscated it?"

Jake nods. "It was the first thing they did."

We've lost a lot of property since we struck out together. Not to mention the solid gold watch that belonged to my father, which fell out of my pocket. Ever since I left home, it's been one thing after another.

"Hey," I say, just realizing something. I can see that I have Jake's attention. "If all of this is true, I mean the blood rain and the earthquake and everything, then that means what's been said about the mark of the beast is true to. That means you *can* lose your soul if you take it."

I can see the blood draining from Jake's face. Like me, this just occurred to him.

Jake gives me a solemn look. "And to think that I almost took it when I was at Raftin. Dang I'm glad I decided not to."

Clifford slams on the breaks. I thrust forward and ram the seat. Oh no, something's wrong.

"What is it," I say.

"Don't know," Jake says. "Let me take a look."

I rise to my feet. I follow closely behind Jake. I want to see what's going on to.

"Someone's standing in the road," Clifford says. "I'd honk the horn if it worked."

Jake is crouched down beside Clifford. I move to the place on the other side of Jake.

"What should we do," I say.

"They look like they need something," Jake says. He turns to Clifford. "Let me go and find out what he wants."

Clifford nods. "Just be careful."

I swallow. "I'm coming with you."

Jake turns on me with a serious look. "No, you're not. Go sit down and I'll take care of this."

I feel my face turning red at Jake's order, like I'm a little kid. He has no right to order me around.

I watch in fear as Jake leaves the bus behind and walks towards the man in the road.

Jake walks up to the man and turns to wave at us. Yeah right, he hasn't convinced me that he's safe.

I wait impatiently as Jake talks to the man. I wonder what the man wants. Why would anyone stand in the middle of the highway?

And then I hear it. A gun. Oh no. Jake.

I look in horror as Jake falls to the highway, clutching his stomach. The man that shot him runs off the road and into a bunch of trees.

I run to the bus door and shout for Clifford to open it for me. And he does.

Oh please dear God don't let him be hurt badly. I set out towards Jake as fast as I can.

As I come up on him, I can already see a bloody spot on his shirt. No.

"Jake," I say, crouching down beside him.

"Kevin," he says, his voice full of fear. "We need to get back to the bus. Help me get up."

"Wait," I say, wanting to check his wound. With shaking hands, I lift up his shirt and see where the bullet grazed him. Oh thank God. He's not hurt as badly as I thought he was. But he's still bleeding pretty badly.

I take his hand and place it over the wound. "You need to try to stop the bleeding," I say.

"Yeah, thanks," he says, struggling to rise to his feet.

"Here," I say, helping him to his feet.

Back on the bus, Jake sits down in the seat across from mine and takes a look at his wound.

"What'd he want," I say.

Jake gives me a weary look. "Money. Only when I told him I didn't have any, he shot me."

"You're lucky," I say, getting Jake's attention. "If that bullet had been a couple inches over, you'd have been in a lot worse shape."

Jake laughs. "Yeah, I don't know how his aim was so poor. We were standing right next to each other."

"Is there anything I can do," Clifford says.

Jake shakes his head. "Just drive. Get out of here fast before he decides to go on a shooting spree."

Clifford nods. "Sure thing."

Without another word, Clifford sets off towards Garbor. I turn back to Jake, who is gritting his teeth from the pain.

"Here," Melody says over my shoulder. She offers Jake something. "It's a pain reliever. It'll help."

"Thanks," Jake says, taking the pill from her. He pops it into his mouth and swallows.

I shake my head inwardly. I just can't believe how many bad things have happened to Jake in the short time I've known him. It's like he's a magnet for bad things.

"We're almost there," I say to Jake. "Just hold on a little longer and you'll get some proper medical care. I'm sure you'll need stitches."

"Stitches," Jake says. "I hope not. I've never had any before. They'll probably hurt."

I sigh. I slide to the end of my seat. I move Jake's shirt aside and look at his wound. It's a good three inches long, and about an inch deep. "Yeah, you'll have to have stitches. Now keep your hand over it," I say. "You don't want to bleed to death."

Jake laughs. "I doubt that's going to happen. No, I'm here to stay."

I laugh. "Until your next calamity."

Jake frowns. "Maybe, maybe not."

I can't help but stare at Jake's finely sculpted abs. I wish I looked as good as he does. One of the first things I plan on doing once we reach Garbor is to find a girlfriend for him. It'll be fun. I bet Jake could have any girl he wants.

Jake clears his throat, getting my attention. "Is there a reason you're staring at my abs?"

I frown. "Yeah, I've never seen anyone with abs like yours before."

"Really," Jake says. "That's odd."

"Not really," I say. "So, ever had a girlfriend, besides Leslie I mean."

Jake laughs. "Yeah, I've had my fair share of girlfriends before. What about you?"

I shake my head. "Nope, not yet."

"You're joking," Jake says.

"Doesn't look like he is," Panvil says, speaking up. Honestly, I almost forgot all about our other friends.

"Let me guess," Panvil says. "The reason you haven't had a girlfriend is because you're too picky."

I point a finger at Panvil. "There it is. You hit the hammer on the nail."

"What about you," I say to Panvil.

Panvil shrugs. "I've had my fair share of girls before. Never married any of them though."

"What about you," Panvil says to Jacob. "Ever had a girlfriend?"

Jacob gives Panvil a cool look. "That's none of your business."

"Fine," Panvil says, throwing his hands up in the air. "Sorry. Jeeze."

"Oh for goodness sake," Clifford says, getting my attention. "What's going on now?"

I turn towards the front of the bus. I see a couple of cars blocking the road ahead.

"Agents," Jake says, taking a look. "Dang it. How are you supposed to make it to Garbor if something tries to stop us every half hour?"

Jake is right. The people blocking the road are agents.

"What do we do," I say.

"Nothing," Jake says. "At least not right now."

I turn to Clifford. "Can you plow through them? I had to do that the other day."

Clifford shakes his head. "It'd be too dangerous. Besides the roads too steep on either side."

"They're motioning for us to get out," Jake says. He turns to me. "I could talk to them, you know, tell them a pack of lies."

I shake my head. "No, absolutely not. Remember, everything in the Bible is true, that means lying is sin."

Jake sighs. "So what would you have me do?"

"Nothing," I say. "Let me try to reason with them. Besides, you're wounded. The last thing we need is for you to start bleeding badly again."

"Fine," Jake says, clearly not happy with this.

"Here," says Melody behind me. I turn around to face her. "Take this rifle. And if they don't see things your way, blast 'em off the road."

"I don't want to kill anyone," I say.

Melody purses her lips together. "But you'll let them kill you, because that's what they're going to do if you don't take the mark of the beast."

"So what would you suggest," I say.

Melody shrugs. "Hard to say. But I'd let them come to us."

Jake seems to like this. "Then that's what we'll do."

I watch with a twinge of fear as an agent comes walking up to the bus. He carries a gun and looks like he means business.

The agent waves a hand at us. "You have five minutes to get off that bus, or we'll blow it off the highway."

I laugh.

"He wasn't joking," Jake says.

"But I don't see...," I say, getting cut off.

"Look beyond the cars," Jake says warily. "See that tank?"

I swallow hard. I nod. This isn't good. I just don't see us getting out of this one.

"Now what do we do," I say, panicking.

Jake gives me a defeated look. "We surrender."

"But we can't," I say. "You know what would happen if we don't take the mark."

"What would you suggest then," Jake says.

I look up at the ceiling. "I don't know," I say. "I guess we can surrender and then try to plan an escape later on. I don't know."

"That's all we *can do* sweetie," Melody says. "We've came as far as we can go together. Now we have to be brave."

I nod.

After running our plan of surrender by Clifford, he actually agrees. "Rather lose my head than my soul," he says glumly.

One by one, we all leave the bus behind. It feels surreal. To think that we nearly made it to Garbor makes it feel even worse.

We all stand in front of the bus. I feel like fear has a huge grip around my chest and is squeezing me. I struggle to take a deep breath.

Boom. Boom. Boom.

I jump backwards as three huge explosions rock the area. I watch in stunned disbelief as both of the agent's cars gets blown off the highway. Next second, the agents bolt off the highway and hide.

As the smoke begins to fade, I see the tank coming towards us. I watch in fear as the tank comes right towards us.

And then it stops.

I swallow hard. What is going on?

A second later, the lid on the top of the tank comes off and someone climbs out.

"It's Donna," Jake says in disbelief. "Or at least it looks like her from this distance."

I watch as the woman jumps down off the tank and lands on the ground. It is Donna.

Without another thought, I run up to her and throw my arms around her.

"Oh thank God," I say.

Donna reciprocates my hug. "Oh Kevin, I thought we'd meet again."

I feel tears forming in my eyes. I just can't believe this.

"How," I say, not able to get anything else out right now.

Donna smiles. "I escaped the agents when their backs were turned. All it took was a minute or so and I was off. Not long after that, I met up with some resistance fighters. They told me they were headed for Garbor, and if I'd like to come. So, here I am."

I swallow hard. "You've been to Garbor," I say.

Donna nods. "Kevin, it's everything we thought it was and then some. You'll love it. Plus, you'll be safe there, I guarantee that."

I introduce Donna to Clifford, who seems delighted to make her acquaintance. Then, I introduce her to Melody and Jacob, who shake her hand warmly.

I shake my head. "I just can't believe this." I give Donna another hug. I hold onto her for a long time.

I back away and let Donna see Jake better.

Donna walks up to Jake. "You're hurt," she says.

"Not bad," Jake says. "It's just a scratch."

Donna pulls Jake into a big hug. I can't help but smile. This is the most amazing thing to ever happen in my life. Well, other than the Rapture of course.

Donna lets go of Jake and takes a step backward. She looks between all of us. "We need to leave quickly before any more agents find us. Follow me and I'll lead you safely to Garbor."

"Is it far," I say.

Donna shakes her head. "No. It's just a few miles up the road."

"Sounds good," I say.

Clifford boards the bus ahead of us. Then the rest of us climbs aboard.

I take my old seat, filled with nervous excitement. If Donna is right, and I think she is, then Garbor is going to be a great city of refuge.

It's so strange. Instead of feeling sleepy, I feel wide awake and alert, like I've just drank a big caffeinated beverage.

I turn to Jake, who looks worried.

I look at his side, where his wound is. The bleeding has started again.

"Keep applying pressure to it," I say. "You're going to have to have stitches, whether you like it or not."

After an hour or so of slow driving behind Donna's tank, we finally arrive at a big gate.

"This is it," Clifford says happily. "We've made it."

I see Donna get out of the tank and motion us to come toward her. Feeling relieved, I get off the bus after Jake and head towards Donna.

Once we get to Donna, she says "now you'll have to show a man your hand to prove that you haven't taken the mark, and then they'll let you in."

Donna leads us up to a small door in the gate. Sure enough, a man asks to see my hand, and so I show it to him. He then tells me to step aside for a moment.

After everyone proves that they haven't taken the mark, the gate slowly begins to open to admit us.

Feeling very happy, I put an arm around Donna and Jake and make my way through the gate.

No sooner than we walk through, I see huge buildings rising up from the ground. Wow. I had no idea that Garbor was this modern. I figured it'd mainly be old buildings that had leaky roofs.

I turn to Jake. "We need to find you a doctor."

Jake lets out a deep sigh. "Fine, if that's what you think, then I'll do it."

"Welcome to Garbor," says a little woman in a bright blue dress.

"Thanks," I say with a smile.

"Kevin," says Donna. "Garbor has some of the best doctors in the country. But they do charge. Do you or your friends have any money?"

I sigh. "No," I say. There's always something.

"But I have a gold coin left," Melody says from behind me.

I turn around to face her.

"Here," Melody says, handing it to me.

"Thanks," I say. I show it to Donna. "Will this work?"

Donna nods. "It should, especially if it's solid gold."

"It is," Melody says.

"Good," Donna says, "because these doctors don't work cheap. Other than that, just about everything else around here is free, believe it or not."

Wow. That sounds good.

I let my hands down off of Donna and Jake. I wipe the sweat off my forehead with the back of my hand. I just can't believe that we're finally here. I hear something slam shut behind us. I turn around to find the gate closed.

Jake gives me a warm smile. "We made it."

I nod. "Thank God."